MYSTERY & FANTASY
STORIES

MYSTERY & FANTASY STORIES

F. SCOTT FITZGERALD

SUGAR SKULL PRESS
LOS ANGELES, CALIFORNIA

TABLE OF STORIES

THE MYSTERY OF THE RAYMOND MORTGAGE

When I first saw John Syrel of the New York Daily News, he was standing before an open window of my house gazing out on the city. It was about six o'clock and the lights were just going on. All down 33rd Street was a long line of gaily illuminated buildings. He was not a tall man, but thanks to the erectness of his posture, and the suppleness of his movement, it would take no athlete to tell that he was of fine build. He was twenty-three years old when I first saw him, and was already a reporter on the News. He was not a handsome man; his face was clean-shaven, and his chin showed him to be of strong character. His eyes and hair were brown.

As I entered the room he turned around slowly and addressed me in a slow, drawling tone: "I think I have the honor of speaking to Mr. Egan, chief of police." I assented, and he went on: "My name is John Syrel and my business—to tell you frankly, is to learn all I can about that case of the Raymond mortgage."

I started to speak but he silenced me with a wave of his hand. "Though I belong to the staff of the Daily News," he continued, "I am not here as an agent of the paper,"

"I am not here," I interrupted coldly, "to tell every newspaper reporter or adventurer about private affairs. James, show this man out."

Syrel turned without a word and I heard his steps echo up the driveway.

However, this was not destined to be the last time I ever saw Syrel, as events will show.

The morning after I first saw John Syrel, I proceeded to the scene of the crime to which he had alluded. On the train I picked up a newspaper and read the following account of the crime and theft, which had followed it:

"EXTRA"

"Great Crime Committed in Suburbs of City"

"Mayor Proceeding to Scenes of Crime"

On the morning of July 1st, a crime and serious theft were committed on the outskirts of the city. Miss Raymond was killed and the body of a servant was found outside of the house. Mr. Raymond of Santuka Lake was awakened on Tuesday morning by a scream and two revolver shots that proceeded from his wife's room. He tried to open the door but it would not open. He was almost certain the door was locked from the inside, when suddenly it swung open disclosing a room in frightful disorder. On the center of the floor was a

8

revolver and on his wife's bed was a bloodstain in the shape of a hand. His wife was missing, but on a closer search he found his daughter under the bed, stone dead. The window was broken in two places. Miss Raymond had a bullet wound on her body and her head was fearfully cut. The body of a servant was found outside with a bullet hole through this head. Mrs. Raymond has not been found.

The room was upset. The bureau drawers were out as if the murderer had been looking for something. Chief of Police Egan is on the scene of the crime, etc., etc.

Just then the conductor called out "Santuka!" The train came to a stop, and getting out of the car I walked up to the house. On the porch I met Gregson, who was supposed to be the ablest detective in the force. He gave me a plan of the house which he said he would like to have me look at before we went in.

"The body of the servant," he said, "is that of John Standish. He has been with family 12 years and was a perfectly honest man. He was only 32 years old."

"The bullet which killed him was not found?" I asked.

"No," he answered; and then, "Well, you had better come in and see for yourself. By the way, there was a fellow hanging around here, who was trying to see the body. When I refused to let him in, he went around to where the servant was shot and I saw him go down on his knees on the grass and begin to search. A few minutes later he stood up and leaned against a tree. Then he came up to the house and asked to see the body again. I said he could if he would go away afterwards. He assented, and when he got inside the room he went down on his knees and under the bed and hunted around. Then he went over to the window and examined the broken pane carefully. After that he declared himself satisfied and went down towards the hotel."

After I had examined the room to my satisfaction, I found that I might as well try to see through a millstone as to try to fathom this mystery. As I finished my investigation I met Gregson in the laboratory.

"I suppose you heard about the mortgage," said he, as we went down stairs. I answered in the negative, and he told me that a valuable mortgage had disappeared from the room in which Miss Raymond was killed. The night before Mr. Raymond had placed the mortgage in a drawer and it had disappeared."

On my way to town that night I met Syrel again, and he bowed cordially to me. I began to feel ashamed of myself for sending him out of my house. As I went into the car the only vacant seat was next to him. I sat down and apologized for my rudeness of the day before. He took it lightly and, there being nothing to say, we sat in silence. At last I ventured a remark.

"What do you think of the case?"

"I don't think anything of it as yet. I haven't had time yet."

Nothing daunted I began again. "Did you learn anything?"

Syrel dug his hand into his pocket and produced a bullet. I examined it.

"Where did you find it?" I asked.

"In the yard," he answered briefly.

At this I again relapsed into my seat. When we reached the city, night was coming on. My first day's investigation was not very successful.

My next day's investigation was no more successful than the first. My friend Syrel was not at home. The maid came into Mr. Raymond's room while I was there and gave notice that she was going to leave. "Mr. Raymond," she said, "there was queer noises outside my window last night. I'd like to stay, sir, but it grates on my nerves." Beyond this nothing happened, and I came home worn out. On the morning of the next day I was awakened by the maid who had a telegram in her hand. I opened it and found it was from Gregson. "Come at once," it said "startling development." I dressed hurriedly and took the first car to Santuka. When I reached the Santuka station, Gregson was waiting for me in a runabout. As soon as I got into the carriage Gregson told me what had happened.

"Someone was in the house last night. You know Mr. Raymond asked me to sleep there. Well, to continue, last night, about one, I began to be very thirsty. I went into the hall to get a drink from the faucet there, and as I was passing from my room (I sleep in Miss Raymond's room) into the hall I heard somebody in Mrs. Raymond's room. Wondering why Mr. Raymond was up at that time of night I went into the sitting room to investigate. I opened the door of Mrs. Raymond's room. The body of Miss Raymond was lying on the sofa. A man was kneeling beside it. His face was away from me, but I could tell by his figure that he was not Mr. Raymond. As I looked he got up softly and I saw him open a bureau. He took something out and put it into his pocket. As he turned around he saw me, and I saw that he was a young man. With a cry of rage he sprang at me, and having no weapon I retreated. He snatched up a heavy Indian club and swung it over my head. I gave a cry which must have alarmed the house, for I know nothing more till I saw Mr. Raymond bending over me."

"How did this man look," I asked. "Would you know him if you saw him again?"

"I think not," he answered, "I only saw his profile."

"The only explanation I can give is this," said I. "The murderer was in Miss Raymond's room and when she came in he overpowered her and inflicted the gash. He then made for Mrs. Raymond's room and carried her off after having first shot Miss Raymond, who attempted to rise. Outside the house he met Standish, who attempted to stop him and was shot."

Gregson smiled. "That solution is impossible," he said.

As we reached the house I saw John Syrel, who beckoned me aside. "If you come with me," he said, "you will learn something that may be valuable to you." I excused myself to Gregson and followed Syrel. As we reached the walk he began to talk.

"Let us suppose that the murderer or murderess escaped from the house. Where would they go? Naturally they wanted to get away. Where did they go? Now, there are two railroad stations near by, Santuka and Lidgeville. I have ascertained that they did not go by Santuka. So did Gregson. I supposed, therefore, that they went by Lidgeville. Gregson didn't; that's the difference. A straight line is the shortest distance between two points. I followed a straight line between here and Lidgeville. At first there was nothing. About two miles farther on I saw some footprints in a marshy hollow. They consisted of three footprints. I took an impression. Here it is. You see this one is a woman's. I have compared it with one of Mrs. Raymond's boots. They are identical. The others are mates. They belong to a man. I compared the bullet I found, where Standish was killed, with one of the remaining cartridges in the revolver that was found in Mrs. Raymond's room. They were mates. Only one shot had been fired and as I had found one bullet, I concluded that either Mrs. or Miss Raymond had fired the shot. I preferred to think Mrs. Raymond fired it because she had fled. Summing these things up and also taking into consideration that Mrs. Raymond must have had some cause to try to kill Standish, I concluded that John Standish killed Miss Raymond through the window of her mother's room, Friday night. I also conclude Mrs. Raymond after ascertaining that her daughter was dead, shot Standish through the window and killed him. Horrified at what she had done she hid behind the door when Mr. Raymond came in.

Then she ran down the back stairs. Going outside she stumbled upon the revolver Standish had used and picking it up took it with her. Somewhere between here and Lidgeville she met the owner of these footprints, either by accident or design and walked with him to the station where they took the early train for Chicago. The stationmaster did not see the man. He says that only a woman bought a ticket, so I concluded that the young man didn't go. Now you must tell me what Gregson told you."

"How did you know all this," exclaimed I astonshed. And then I told him about the midnight visitor. He did not appear to be much astonished, and he said "I guess that the young man is our friend of the footprints. Now you had better go get a brace of revolvers and pack your suitcase if you wish to go with me to find this young man and Mrs. Raymond, whom I think is with him.

Greatly surprised at what I had heard I took the first train back to town. I bought a pair of fine Colt revolvers, a dark lantern, and two changes of clothing. We went over to Lidgeville and found that a young man had left on the six o'clock train for Ithaca. On reaching Ithaca we found that he had changed trains and was now half way to Princeton, New Jersey. It was five o'clock, but we took a fast train and expected to overtake him half way between Ithaca and Princeton. What was our chagrin when on reaching the slow train, to find he had gotten off at Indianous and was now probably safe. Thoroughly disappointed we took the train for Indianous. The ticket seller said that a young man in a light gray suit had taken a bus to the Raswell Hotel. We found the bus that the stationmaster said he had taken, in the street. We went up to the driver and he admitted that he had started for the Raswell Hotel in his cab.

"But," said the old fellow, "when I reached there, the fellow had clean disappeared, an' I never got his fare."

Syrel groaned; it was plain that we had lost the young man. We took the next train for New York and telegraphed to Mr. Raymond that we would be down Monday. Sunday night, however, I was called to the phone and recognized Syrel's voice. He directed me to come at once to five hundred thirty-four Chestnut Street. I met him on the doorstep.

"What have you heard?" I asked.

"I have an agent in Indianous," he replied, "in the shape of an Arab boy whom I employ for 10 cents a day. I told him to spot the woman and to-day I got a telegram from him (I left him money to send one), saying to come at once. So come on."

We took the train for Indianous. "Smidy," the young Arab, met us at the station.

"You see, sur, it's dis way. You says, 'Spot de guy wid dat hack,' and I says I would. Dat night a young dude comes out of er house on Pine Street and give the cabman a $10 bill. An den he went back into the house and a minute after he comes out wid a woman, an' den day went down here a little way an' goes into a house farther down the street, I'll show you de place."

We followed Smidy down the street until we arrived at a corner house. The ground floor was occupied by a cigar store, but the second floor was evidently for rent. As we stood there a face appeared at the window and, seeing us, hastily retreated. Syrel pulled a picture from his pocket. "It's she," he exclaimed, and calling us to follow he dashed into a little side door. We heard voices upstairs, a shuffle of feet and a noise as if a door had been shut.

"Up the stairs," shouted Syrel, and we followed him, taking two steps at a bound. As we reached the top landing we were met by a young man.

"What right have you to enter this house?" he demanded.

"The right of the law," replied Syrel.

"I didn't do it" broke out the young man. "It was this way. Agnes Raymond loved me—she did not love Standish—he shot her; and God did not let her murder go unrevenged. It was well Mrs. Raymond killed him, for his blood would have been on my hands. I went back to see Agnes before she was buried. A man came in. I knocked him down. I didn't know until a moment ago that Mrs. Raymond had killed him.

"I forgot Mrs. Raymond" screamed Syrel, "where is she?"

"She is out of your power forever," said the young man.

Syrel brushed past him and, with Smidy and I following, burst open the door of the room at the head of the stairs. We rushed in.

On the floor lay a woman, and as soon as I touched her heart I knew she was beyond the doctor's skill.

"She has taken poison," I said. Syre looked around, the young man had gone. And we stood there aghast in the presence of death.

TARQUIN OF CHEAPSIDE

Running footsteps—light, soft-soled shoes made of curious leathery cloth brought from Ceylon setting the pace; thick flowing boots, two pairs, dark blue and gilt, reflecting the moonlight in blunt gleams and splotches, following a stone's throw behind.

Soft Shoes flashes through a patch of moonlight, then darts into a blind labyrinth of alleys and becomes only an intermittent scuffle ahead somewhere in the enfolding darkness. In go Flowing Boots, with short swords lurching and long plumes awry, finding a breath to curse God and the black lanes of London.

Soft Shoes leaps a shadowy gate and crackles through a hedgerow. Flowing Boots leap the gate and crackle through the hedgerow—and there, startlingly, is the watch ahead—two murderous pikemen of ferocious cast of mouth acquired in Holland and the Spanish marches.

But there is no cry for help. The pursued does not fall panting at the feet of the watch, clutching a purse; neither do the pursuers raise a hue and cry. Soft Shoes goes by in a rush of swift air. The watch curse and hesitate, glance after the fugitive, and then spread their pikes grimly across the road and wait for Flowing Boots.

Darkness, like a great hand, cuts off the even flow of the moon.

The hand moves off the moon whose pale caress finds again the eaves and lintels, and the watch, wounded and tumbled in the dust. Up the street one of Flowing Boots leaves a black trail of spots until he binds himself, clumsily as he runs, with fine lace caught from his throat.

It was no affair for the watch: Satan was at large tonight and Satan seemed to be he who appeared dimly in front, heel over gate, knee over fence. Moreover, the adversary was obviously traveling near home or at least in that section of London consecrated to his coarser whims, for the street narrowed like a road in a picture and the houses bent over further and further, cooping in natural ambushes suitable for murder and its histrionic sister, sudden death.

Down long and sinuous lanes twisted the hunted and the harriers, always in and out of the moon in a perpetual queen's move over a checkerboard of glints and patches. Ahead, the quarry, minus his leather jerkin now and half blinded by drips of sweat, had taken to scanning his ground desperately on both sides. As a result he suddenly slowed short, and retracing his steps a bit scooted up an alley so dark that it seemed that here sun and moon had been in eclipse since the last glacier slipped roaring over the earth. Two hundred yards down he stopped and crammed himself into a niche in the wall where he huddled and panted silently, a grotesque god without bulk or outline in the gloom.

Flowing Boots, two pairs, drew near, came up, went by, halted twenty yards beyond him, and spoke in deep-lunged, scanty whispers:

"I was attune to that scuffle; it stopped."

"Within twenty paces."

"He's hid."

"Stay together now and we'll cut him up."

The voice faded into a low crunch of a boot, nor did Soft Shoes wait to hear more—he sprang in three leaps across the alley, where he bounded up, flapped for a moment on the top of the wall like a huge bird, and disappeared, gulped down by the hungry night at a mouthful.

II

He read at wine, he read in bed, He read aloud, had he the breath, His every thought was with the dead, And so he read himself to death.

Any visitor to the old James the First graveyard near Peat's Hill may spell out this bit of doggerel, undoubtedly one of the worst recorded of an Elizabethan, on the tomb of Weasel Caster.

This death of his, says the antiquary, occurred when he was thirty-seven, but as this story is concerned with the night of a certain chase through darkness, we find him still alive, still reading. His eyes were somewhat dim, his stomach somewhat obvious—he was a misbuilt man and indolent—oh, Heavens! But an era is an era, and in the reign of Elizabeth, by the grace of Luther, Queen of England, no man could help but catch the spirit of enthusiasm. Every loft in Cheapside published its *Magnum Folium* (or magazine) of the new blank verse; the Cheapside Players would produce anything on sight as long as it "got away from those reactionary miracle plays," and the English Bible had run through seven "very large" printings in as many months.

So Wessel Caxter (who in his youth had gone to sea) was now a reader of all on which he could lay his hands—he read manuscripts in holy friendship; he dined rotten poets; he loitered about the shops where the *Magna Folia* were printed, and he listened tolerantly while the young playwrights wrangled and bickered among themselves, and behind each other's backs made bitter and malicious charges of plagiarism or anything else they could think of.

Tonight he had a book, a piece of work that, though inordinately versed, contained, he thought, some rather excellent political satire. *The Faerie Queene* by Edmund Spenser lay before him under the tremulous candlelight. He had ploughed through a canto; he was beginning another:

THE LEGEND OF BRITOMARTIS or of CHASTITY

It fails me here to write of Chastity. The fayrest vertue, far above the rest...

A sudden rush of feet on the stairs, a rusty swing-open of the thin door, and a man thrust himself into the room, a man without a jerkin, panting, sobbing, on the verge of collapse.

"Wessel," words choked him, "stick me away somewhere, love of Our Lady!"

Caxter rose, carefully closing his book, and bolted the door in some concern.

"I'm pursued," cried out Soft Shoes. "I vow there's two short-witted blades trying to make me into mincemeat and near succeeding. They saw me hop the back wall!"

"It would need," said Wessel, looking at him curiously, "several battalions armed with blunderbusses, and two or three Armadas, to keep you reasonably secure from the revenges of the world."

Soft Shoes smiled with satisfaction. His sobbing gasps were giving way to quick, precise breathing; his hunted air had faded to a faintly perturbed irony.

"I feel little surprise," continued Wessel.

"They were two such dreary apes."

"Making a total of three."

"Only two unless you stick me away. Man, man, come Alive; they'll be on the stairs in a spark's age."

Wessel took a dismantled pikestaff from the corner, and raising it to the high ceiling, dislodged a rough trapdoor opening into a garret above.

"There's no ladder."

He moved a bench under the trap, upon which Soft Shoes mounted, crouched, hesitated, crouched again, and then leaped amazingly upward. He caught at the edge of the aperture and swung back and forth for a moment, shifting his hold; finally doubled up and disappeared into the darkness above. There was a scurry, a migration of rats, as the trap door was replaced...silence.

Wessel returned to his reading table, opened to the Legend of Britomartis or of Chastity—and waited.

Almost a minute later there was a scramble on the stairs and an intolerable hammering at the door. Weasel sighed and, picking up his candle, rose.

"Who's there?"

"Open the door!"

"Who's there?"

An aching blow frightened the frail wood, splintered it around the edge. Weasel opened it a scarce three inches, and held the candle high. His was to play the timorous, the super-respectable citizen, disgracefully disturbed.

"One small hour of the night for rest. Is that too much to ask from every brawler and—"

"Quiet, gossip! Have you seen a perspiring fellow?"

The shadows of two gallants fell in immense wavering outlines over the narrow stairs; by the light Weasel scrutinized them closely. Gentlemen, they were, hastily but richly dressed—one of them wounded severely in the hand, both radiating a sort of furious horror. Waving aside Wessel's ready miscomprehension, they pushed by him into the room and with their swords went through the business of poking carefully into all suspected dark spots in the room, further extending their search to Wessel's bedchamber.

"Is he hid here?" demanded the wounded man fiercely.

"Is who here?"

"Any man but you."

"Only two others that I know of."

For a second Wessel feared that he had been too damned funny, for the gallants made as though to prick him through.

"I heard a man on the stairs," he said hastily, "full five minutes ago, it was. He most certainly failed to come up."

He went on to explain his absorption in *The Faerie Queene* but, for the moment at least, his visitors, like the great saints, were anaesthetic to culture.

"What's been done?" inquired Wessel.

"Violence!" said the man with the wounded hand. Wessel noticed that his eyes were quite wild. "My own sister. Oh, Christ in heaven, give us this man!"

Wessel winced.

"Who is the man?"

"God's word! We know not even that. What's that trap up there?" he added suddenly.

"It's nailed down. It's not been used for years." He thought of the pole in the corner and quailed in his belly, but the utter despair of the two men dulled their astuteness.

"It would take a ladder for any one not a tumbler," said the wounded man listlessly.

His companion broke into hysterical laughter.

"A tumbler. Oh, a tumbler. Oh—"

Wessel stared at them in wonder.

"That appeals to my most tragic humor," cried the man, "that no one—oh, no one—could get up there but a tumbler."

The gallant with the wounded hand snapped his good fingers impatiently.

"We must go next door—and then on—"

26

Helplessly they went as two walking under a dark and storm-swept sky.

Wessel closed and bolted the door and stood a moment by it, frowning in pity. A low-breathed "Ha!" made him look up. Soft Shoes had already raised the trap and was looking down into the room, his rather elfish face squeezed into a grimace, half of distaste, half of sardonic amusement.

"They take off their heads with their helmets," he remarked in a whisper, "but as for you and me, Wessel, we are two cunning men."

"Now you be cursed," cried Wessel vehemently. "I knew you for a dog, but when I hear even the half of a tale like this, I know you for such a dirty cur that I am minded to club your skull."

Soft Shoes stared at him, blinking.

"At all events," he replied finally, "I find dignity impossible in this position."

With this he let his body through the trap, hung for an instant, and dropped the seven feet to the floor.

"There was a rat considered my ear with the air of a gourmet," he continued, dusting his hands on his breeches. "I told him in the rat's peculiar idiom that I was deadly poison, so he took himself off."

"Let's hear of this night's lechery!" insisted Wessel angrily.

Soft Shoes touched his thumb to his nose and wiggled the fingers derisively at Wessel.

"Street gamin!" muttered Wessel.

"Have you any paper?" demanded Soft Shoes irrelevantly, and then rudely added, "or can yon write?"

"Why should I give you paper?"

"You wanted to hear of the night's entertainment. So you shall, an you give me pen, ink, a sheaf of paper, and a room to myself."

Wessel hesitated.

"Get out!" he said finally.

"As you will. Yet you have missed a most intriguing story."

Wessel wavered—he was soft as taffy, that man—gave in. Soft Shoes went into the adjoining room with the begrudged writing materials and precisely dosed the door. Wessel grunted and returned to *The Faerie Queene*; so silence came once more upon the house.

III

Three o'clock went into four. The room paled, the dark outside was shot through with damp and chill, and Wessel, cupping his brain in his hands, bent low over his table, tracing through the pattern of knights and fairies and the harrowing distresses of many girls. There were dragons chortling along the narrow street outside; when the sleepy armorer's boy began his work at half-past five the heavy clink and chank of plate and linked mail swelled to the echo of a marching cavalcade.

A fog shut down at the first flare of dawn, and the room was grayish yellow at six when Wessel tiptoed to his cupboard bedchamber and pulled open the door. His guest turned on him a face pale as parchment m which two distraught eyes burned like great red letters. He had drawn a chair close to Wessel's *prie-dieu* winch he was using as a desk; and on it was an amazing stack of closely written pages. With a long sigh Wessel withdrew and returned to his siren, calling himself fool for not claiming his bed here at dawn.

The clump of boots outside, the croaking of old beldames from attic to attic, the dull murmur of morning, unnerved him, and, dozing, he slumped in his chair, his brain, overladen with sound and color, working intolerably over the imagery that stacked it. In this restless dream of his he was one of a thousand groaning bodies crashed near the sun, a helpless bridge for the strong-eyed Apollo. The dream tore at him, scraped along his mind like a ragged knife. When a hot hand touched his shoulder, he awoke with what was nearly a scream to find the fog thick in the room and his guest, a gray ghost of misty stuff, beside him with a pile of paper in his hand.

"It should be a most intriguing tale, I believe, though it requires some going over. May I ask you to lock it away, and in God's name let me sleep?"

He waited for no answer, but thrust the pile at Wessel, and literally poured himself like stuff from a suddenly inverted bottle upon a couch in the corner; slept, with his breathing regular, but his brow wrinkled in a curious and somewhat uncanny manner.

Wessel yawned sleepily and, glancing at the scrawled, uncertain first page, he began reading aloud very softly:

The Rape of Lucrece

From the besieged Ardea all in post, Borne by the trustless wings of false desire, Lust-breathed Tarquin leaves the Roman host—

THE CURIOUS CASE OF
BENJAMIN BUTTON

I

As long ago as 1860 it was the proper thing to be born at home. At present, so I am told, the high gods of medicine have decreed that the first cries of the young shall be uttered upon the anaesthetic air of a hospital, preferably a fashionable one. So young Mr. and Mrs. Roger Button were fifty years ahead of style when they decided, one day in the summer of 1860, that their first baby should be born in a hospital. Whether this anachronism had any bearing upon the astonishing history I am about to set down will never be known.

I shall tell you what occurred, and let you judge for yourself.

The Roger Buttons held an enviable position, both social and financial, in antebellum Baltimore. They were related to the This Family and the That Family, which, as every Southerner knew, entitled them to membership in that enormous peerage which largely populated the Confederacy. This was their first experience with the charming old custom of having babies—Mr. Button was naturally nervous. He hoped it would be a boy so that he could be sent to Yale College in

Connecticut, at which institution Mr. Button himself had been known for four years by the somewhat obvious nickname of "Cuff."

On the September morning consecrated to the enormous event he arose nervously at six o'clock dressed himself, adjusted an impeccable stock, and hurried forth through the streets of Baltimore to the hospital, to determine whether the darkness of the night had borne in new life upon its bosom.

When he was approximately a hundred yards from the Maryland Private Hospital for Ladies and Gentlemen he saw Doctor Keene, the family physician, descending the front steps, rubbing his hands together with a washing movement—as all doctors are required to do by the unwritten ethics of their profession.

Mr. Roger Button, the president of Roger Button & Co., Wholesale Hardware, began to run toward Doctor Keene with much less dignity than was expected from a Southern gentleman of that picturesque period.

"Doctor Keene!" he called. "Oh, Doctor Keene!"

The doctor heard him, faced around, and stood waiting, a curious expression settling on his harsh, medicinal face as Mr. Button drew near.

"What happened?" demanded Mr. Button, as he came up in a gasping rush.

"What was it? How is she? A boy? Who is it? What—"

"Talk sense!" said Doctor Keene sharply, He appeared somewhat irritated.

"Is the child born?" begged Mr. Button.

Doctor Keene frowned. "Why, yes, I suppose so—after a fashion." Again he threw a curious glance at Mr. Button.

"Is my wife all right?"

"Yes."

"Is it a boy or a girl?"

"Here now!" cried Doctor Keene in a perfect passion of irritation, "I'll ask you to go and see for yourself. Outrageous!" He snapped the last word out in almost one syllable, then he turned away muttering: "Do you imagine a case like this will help my professional reputation? One more would ruin me—ruin anybody."

"What's the matter?" demanded Mr. Button appalled. "Triplets?"

"No, not triplets!" answered the doctor cuttingly. "What's more, you can go and see for yourself. And get another doctor. I brought you into the world, young man, and I've been physician to your family for forty years, but I'm through with you! I don't want to see you or any of your relatives ever again! Goodbye!"

Then he turned sharply, and without another word climbed into his phaeton, which was waiting at the curbstone, and drove severely away.

Mr. Button stood there upon the sidewalk, stupefied and trembling from head to foot. What horrible mishap had occurred? He had suddenly lost all desire to go into the Maryland Private Hospital for Ladies and Gentlemen—it was with the greatest difficulty that, a moment later, he forced himself to mount the steps and enter the front door.

A nurse was sitting behind a desk in the opaque gloom of the hall. Swallowing his shame, Mr. Button approached her.

"Good morning," she remarked, looking up at him pleasantly.

"Good morning. I—I am Mr. Button."

At this a look of utter terror spread itself over girl's face. She rose to her feet and seemed about to fly from the hall, restraining herself only with the most apparent difficulty.

"I want to see my child," said Mr. Button.

The nurse gave a little scream. "Oh—of course!" she cried hysterically. "Upstairs. Right upstairs. Go—*up!*"

She pointed the direction, and Mr. Button, bathed in cool perspiration, turned falteringly, and began to mount to the second floor. In the upper hall he addressed another nurse who approached him, basin in hand. "I'm Mr. Button," he managed to articulate. "I want to see my—"

Clank! The basin clattered to the floor and rolled in the direction of the stairs. Clank! Clank! It began a methodical descent as if sharing in the general terror that this gentleman provoked.

"I want to see my child!" Mr. Button almost shrieked. He was on the verge of collapse.

Clank! The basin reached the first floor. The nurse regained control of herself, and threw Mr. Button a look of hearty contempt.

"All *right*, Mr. Button," she agreed in a hushed voice. "Very *well!* But if you *knew* what a state it's put us all in this morning! It's perfectly outrageous! The hospital will never have a ghost of a reputation after—"

"Hurry!" he cried hoarsely. "I can't stand this!"

"Come this way, then, Mr. Button."

He dragged himself after her. At the end of a long hall they reached a room from which proceeded a variety of howls—indeed, a room that, in later parlance, would have been known as the "crying room." They entered.

"Well," gasped Mr. Button, "which is mine?"

"There!" said the nurse.

Mr. Button's eyes followed her pointing finger, and this is what he saw. Wrapped in a voluminous white blanket, and partly crammed into one of the cribs, there sat an old man apparently about seventy years of age. His sparse hair was almost white, and from his chin dripped a long smoke-colored beard, which waved absurdly back and forth, fanned by the breeze coming in at the window. He looked up at Mr. Button with dim, faded eyes in which lurked a puzzled question.

"Am I mad?" thundered Mr. Button, his terror resolving into rage. "Is this some ghastly hospital joke?

"It doesn't seem like a joke to us," replied the nurse severely. "And I don't know whether you're mad or not—but that is most certainly your child."

The cool perspiration redoubled on Mr. Button's forehead. He closed his eyes, and then, opening them, looked again. There was no mistake—he was gazing at a man of threescore and ten—a *baby* of threescore and ten, a baby whose feet hung over the sides of the crib in which it was reposing.

The old man looked placidly from one to the other for a moment, and then suddenly spoke in a cracked and ancient voice. "Are you my father?" he demanded.

Mr. Button and the nurse started violently.

"Because if you are," went on the old man querulously, "I wish you'd get me out of this place—or, at least, get them to put a comfortable rocker in here."

"Where in God's name did you come from? Who are you?" burst out Mr. Button frantically.

"I can't tell you *exactly* who I am," replied the querulous whine, "because I've only been born a few hours—but my last name is certainly Button."

"You lie! You're an impostor!"

The old man turned wearily to the nurse. "Nice way to welcome a newborn child," he complained in a weak voice. "Tell him he's wrong, why don't you?"

"You're wrong. Mr. Button," said the nurse severely. "This is your child, and you'll have to make the best of it. We're going to ask you to take him home with you as soon as possible— sometime today."

"Home?" repeated Mr. Button incredulously.

"Yes, we can't have him here. We really can't, you know?"

"I'm right glad of it," whined the old man. "This is a fine place to keep a youngster of quiet tastes. With all this yelling and howling, I haven't been able to get a wink of sleep. I asked for something to eat"—here his voice rose to a shrill note of protest—"and they brought me a bottle of milk!"

Mr. Button, sank down upon a chair near his son and concealed his face in his hands. "My heavens!" he murmured, in an ecstasy of horror. "What will people say? What must I do?"

"You'll have to take him home," insisted the nurse—"immediately!"

A grotesque picture formed itself with dreadful clarity before the eyes of the tortured man—a picture of himself walking through the crowded streets of the city with this appalling apparition stalking by his side.

"I can't. I can't," he moaned.

People would stop to speak to him, and what was he going to say? He would have to introduce this—this septuagenarian: "This is my son, born early this morning." And then the old man would gather his blanket around him and they would plod on, past the bustling stores, the slave market—for a dark instant Mr. Button wished passionately that his son was black—past the luxurious houses of the residential district, past the home for the aged…

"Come! Pull yourself together," commanded the nurse.

"See here," the old man announced suddenly, "if you think I'm going to walk home in this blanket, you're entirely mistaken."

"Babies always have blankets."

With a malicious crackle the old man held up a small white swaddling garment. "Look!" he quavered. "*This* is what they had ready for me."

"Babies always wear those," said the nurse primly.

"Well," said the old man, "this baby's not going to wear anything in about two minutes. This blanket itches. They might at least have given me a sheet."

"Keep it on! Keep it on!" said Mr. Button hurriedly. He turned to the nurse. "What'll I do?"

"Go down town and buy your son some clothes."

Mr. Button's son's voice followed him down into the hall: "And a cane, father. I want to have a cane."

Mr. Button banged the outer door savagely....

"Good morning," Mr. Button said nervously, to the clerk in the Chesapeake Dry Goods Company. "I want to buy some clothes for my child."

"How old is your child, sir?"

"About six hours," answered Mr. Button, without due consideration.

"Babies' supply department in the rear."

"Why, I don't think—I'm not sure that's what I want. It's—he's an unusually large-size child. Exceptionally—ah large."

"They have the largest child's sizes."

"Where is the boys' department?" inquired Mr. Button, shifting his ground desperately. He felt that the clerk must surely scent his shameful secret.

"Right here."

"Well—" He hesitated. The notion of dressing his son in men's clothes was repugnant to him. If, say, he could only find a very large boy's suit, he might cut off that long and awful beard, dye the white hair brown, and thus manage to conceal the worst, and to retain something of his own self-respect—not to mention his position in Baltimore society.

But a frantic inspection of the boys' department revealed no suits to fit the newborn Button. He blamed the store, of course—in such cases it is the thing to blame the store.

"How old did you say that boy of yours was?" demanded the clerk curiously.

"He's—sixteen."

"Oh, I beg your pardon. I thought you said six *hours*. You'll find the youths' department in the next aisle."

Mr. Button turned miserably away. Then he stopped, brightened, and pointed his finger toward a dressed dummy in the window display. "There!" he exclaimed. "I'll take that suit, out there on the dummy."

The clerk stared. "Why," he protested, "that's not a child's suit. At least it *is*, but it's for fancy dress. You could wear it yourself!"

"Wrap it up," insisted his customer nervously. "That's what I want."

The astonished clerk obeyed.

Back at the hospital Mr. Button entered the nursery and almost threw the package at his son. "Here's your clothes," he snapped out.

The old man untied the package and viewed the contents with a quizzical eye.

"They look sort of funny to me," he complained, "I don't want to be made a monkey of—"

"You've made a monkey of me!" retorted Mr. Button fiercely. "Never you mind how funny you look. Put them on—or I'll—or I'll *spank* you." He swallowed uneasily at the penultimate word, feeling nevertheless that it was the proper thing to say.

"All right, father"—this with a grotesque simulation of filial respect—"you've lived longer; you know best. Just as you say."

As before, the sound of the word "father" caused Mr. Button to start violently.

"And hurry."

"I'm hurrying, father."

When his son was dressed Mr. Button regarded him with depression. The costume consisted of dotted socks, pink pants, and a belted blouse with a wide white collar. Over the latter waved the long whitish beard, drooping almost to the waist. The effect was not good.

"Wait!"

Mr. Button seized a hospital shears and with three quick snaps amputated a large section of the beard. But even with this improvement the ensemble fell far short of perfection. The remaining brush of scraggly hair, the watery eyes, the ancient teeth, seemed oddly out of tone with the gaiety of the costume. Mr. Button, however, was obdurate—he held out his hand. "Come along!" he said sternly.

His son took the hand trustingly. "What are you going to call me, dad?" he quavered as they walked from the nursery—"just 'baby' for a while? till you think of a better name?"

Mr. Button grunted. "I don't know," he answered harshly. "I think we'll call you Methuselah."

Even after the new addition to the Button family had had his hair cut short and then dyed to a sparse unnatural black, had had his face shaved so close that it glistened, and had been attired in small-boy clothes made to order by a flabbergasted tailor, it was impossible for Button to ignore the fact that his son was a poor excuse for a first family baby. Despite his aged stoop, Benjamin Button—for it was by this name they called him instead of by the appropriate but invidious Methuselah—was five feet eight inches tall. His clothes did not conceal this, nor did the clipping and dyeing of his eyebrows disguise the fact that the eyes under—were faded and watery and tired. In fact, the baby nurse who had been engaged in advance left the house after one look, in a state of considerable indignation.

But Mr. Button persisted in his unwavering purpose. Benjamin was a baby, and a baby he should remain. At first he declared that if Benjamin didn't like warm milk he could go without food altogether, but he was finally prevailed upon to allow his son bread and butter, and even oatmeal by way of a compromise. One day he brought home a rattle and, giving it to Benjamin, insisted in no uncertain terms that he should "play with it," whereupon the old man took it with—a weary expression and could be heard jingling it obediently at intervals throughout the day.

There can be no doubt, though, that the rattle bored him, and that he found other and more soothing amusements when he was left alone. For instance, Mr. Button discovered one day that during the preceding week he had smoked more cigars than ever before—a phenomenon, which was explained a few days later when, entering the nursery unexpectedly, he found the room full of faint blue haze and Benjamin, with a guilty expression on his face, trying to conceal the butt of a dark Havana. This, of course, called for a severe spanking, but Mr. Button found that he could not bring himself to administer it. He merely warned his son that he would "stunt his growth."

Nevertheless he persisted in his attitude. He brought home lead soldiers, he brought toy trains, he brought large pleasant animals made of cotton, and, to perfect the illusion which he was creating—for himself at least—he passionately demanded of the clerk in the toy store whether "the paint would come oft the pink duck if the baby put it in his mouth." But, despite all his father's efforts, Benjamin refused to be interested. He would steal down the back stairs and return to the nursery with a volume of the Encyclopedia Britannica, over which he would pore through an afternoon, while his cotton cows and his Noah's ark were left neglected on the floor. Against such a stubbornness Mr. Button's efforts were of little avail.

The sensation created in Baltimore was, at first, prodigious. What the mishap would have cost the Buttons and their kinsfolk socially cannot be determined, for the outbreak of the Civil War drew the city's attention to other things. A few people who were unfailingly polite racked their brains for compliments to give to the parents— and finally hit upon the ingenious device of declaring that the baby resembled his grandfather, a fact which, due to the standard state of decay common to all men of seventy, could not be denied. Mr. and Mrs. Roger Button were not pleased, and Benjamin's grandfather was furiously insulted.

Benjamin, once he left the hospital, took life as he found it. Several small boys were brought to see him, and he spent a stiff-jointed afternoon trying to work up an interest in tops and marbles— he even managed, quite accidentally, to break a kitchen window with a stone from a sling shot, a feat which secretly delighted his father.

Thereafter Benjamin contrived to break something every day, but he did these things only because they were expected of him, and because he was by nature obliging.

When his grandfather's initial antagonism wore off, Benjamin and that gentleman took enormous pleasure in one another's company. They would sit for hours, these two, so far apart in age and experience, and, like old cronies, discuss with tireless monotony the slow events of the day. Benjamin felt more at ease in his grandfather's presence than in his parents'—they seemed always somewhat in awe of him and, despite the dictatorial authority they exercised over him, frequently addressed him as "Mr."

He was as puzzled as any one else at the apparently advanced age of his mind and body at birth. He read up on it in the medical journal, but found that no such case had been previously recorded. At his father's urging he made an honest attempt to play with other boys, and frequently he joined in the milder games—football shook him up too much, and he feared that in case of a fracture his ancient bones would refuse to knit.

When he was five he was sent to kindergarten, where he initiated into the art of pasting green paper on orange paper, of weaving colored maps and manufacturing eternal cardboard necklaces. He was inclined to drowse off to sleep in the middle of these tasks, a habit which both irritated and frightened his young teacher. To his relief she complained to his parents, and he was removed from the school. The Roger Buttons told their friends that they felt he was too young.

By the time he was twelve years old his parents had grown used to him. Indeed, so strong is the force of custom that they no longer felt that he was different from any other child—except when some curious anomaly reminded them of the fact. But one day a few weeks after his twelfth birthday, while looking in the mirror, Benjamin made, or thought he made, an astonishing discovery. Did his eyes deceive him, or had his hair turned in the dozen years of his life from white to iron-gray under its concealing dye? Was the network of wrinkles on his face becoming less pronounced? Was his skin healthier and firmer, with even a touch of ruddy winter color? He could not tell. He knew that he no longer stooped, and that his physical condition had improved since the early days of his life.

"Can it be—?" he thought to himself, or, rather, scarcely dared to think.

He went to his father. "I am grown," he announced determinedly. "I want to put on long trousers."

His father hesitated. "Well," he said finally, "I don't know. Fourteen is the age for putting on long trousers—and you are only twelve."

"But you'll have to admit," protested Benjamin, "that I'm big for my age."

His father looked at him with illusory speculation. "Oh, I'm not so sure of that," he said. "I was as big as you when I was twelve."

This was not true—it was all part of Roger Button's silent agreement with himself to believe in his son's normality.

Finally a compromise was reached. Benjamin was to continue to dye his hair. He was to make a better attempt to play with boys of his own age. He was not to wear his spectacles or carry a cane in the street. In return for these concessions he was allowed his first suit of long trousers...

Of the life of Benjamin Button between his twelfth and twenty-first year I intend to say little. Suffice to record that they were years of normal ungrowth. When Benjamin was eighteen he was erect as a man of fifty; he had more hair and it was of a dark gray; his step was firm, his voice had lost its cracked quaver and descended to a healthy baritone. So his father sent him up to Connecticut to take examinations for entrance to Yale College. Benjamin passed his examination and became a member of the freshman class.

On the third day following his matriculation he received a notification from Mr. Hart, the college registrar, to call at his office and arrange his schedule. Benjamin, glancing in the mirror, decided that his hair needed a new application of its brown dye, but an anxious inspection of his bureau drawer disclosed that the dye bottle was not there. Then he remembered—he had emptied it the day before and thrown it away.

He was in a dilemma. He was due at the registrar's in five minutes. There seemed to be no help for it—he must go as he was. He did.

"Good-morning," said the registrar politely. "You've come to inquire about your son."

"Why, as a matter of fact, my name's Button—" began Benjamin, but Mr. Hart cut him off.

"I'm very glad to meet you, Mr. Button. I'm expecting your son here any minute."

"That's me!" burst out Benjamin. "I'm a freshman."

"What!"

"I'm a freshman."

"Surely you're joking."

"Not at all."

The registrar frowned and glanced at a card before him. "Why, I have Mr. Benjamin Button's age down here as eighteen."

"That's my age," asserted Benjamin, flushing slightly.

The registrar eyed him wearily. "Now surely, Mr. Button, you don't expect me to believe that."

Benjamin smiled wearily. "I am eighteen," he repeated.

The registrar pointed sternly to the door. "Get out," he said. "Get out of college and get out of town. You are a dangerous lunatic."

"I am eighteen."

Mr. Hart opened the door. "The idea!" he shouted. "A man of your age trying to enter here as a freshman. Eighteen years old, are you? Well, I'll give you eighteen minutes to get out of town."

Benjamin Button walked with dignity from the room, and half a dozen undergraduates, who were waiting in the hall, followed him curiously with their eyes. When he had gone a little way he turned around, faced the infuriated registrar, who was still standing in the door-way, and repeated in a firm voice: "I am eighteen years old."

To a chorus of titters that went up from the group of undergraduates, Benjamin walked away.

But he was not fated to escape so easily. On his melancholy walk to the railroad station he found that he was being followed by a group, then by a swarm, and finally by a dense mass of under-graduates. The word had gone around that a luna-tic had passed the entrance examinations for Yale and attempted to palm himself off as a youth of eighteen. A fever of excitement permeated the col-lege. Men ran hatless out of classes, the football team abandoned its practice and joined the mob, professors' wives with bonnets awry and bustles out of position, ran shouting after the procession, from which proceeded a continual succession of remarks aimed at the tender sensibilities of Benjamin Button.

"He must be the wandering Jew!"

"He ought to go to prep school at his age!"

"Look at the infant prodigy!"

"He thought this was the old men's home."

"Go up to Harvard!"

Benjamin increased his gait, and soon he was running. He would show them! He *would* go to Harvard, and then they would regret these ill-considered taunts!

Safely on board the train for Baltimore, he put his head from the window. "You'll regret this!" he shouted.

"Ha-ha!" the undergraduates laughed. "Ha-ha-ha!" It was the biggest mistake that Yale College had ever made....

In 1880 Benjamin Button was twenty years old, and he signalized his birthday by going to work for his father in Roger Button & Co., Wholesale Hardware. It was in that same year that he began "going out socially"—that is, his father insisted on taking him to several fashionable dances. Roger Button was now fifty, and he and his son were more and more companion-able—in fact, since Benjamin had ceased to dye his hair (which was still grayish) they appeared about the same age, and could have passed for brothers.

One night in August they got into the phaeton attired in their full-dress suits and drove out to a dance at the Shevlins' country house, situated just outside of Baltimore. It was a gorgeous evening. A full moon drenched the road to the lusterless color of platinum, and late-blooming harvest flowers breathed into the motionless air aromas that were like low, half-heard laughter. The open country, carpeted for rods around with bright wheat, was translucent as in the day. It was al-most impossible not to be affected by the sheer beauty of the sky—almost.

"There's a great future in the dry-goods busi-ness," Roger Button was saying. He was not a spiritual man—his aesthetic sense was rudimen-tary.

"Old fellows like me can't learn new tricks," he observed profoundly. "It's you youngsters with energy and vitality that have the great future before you."

Far up the road the lights of the Shevlins' country house drifted into view, and presently there was a sighing sound that crept persistently toward them—it might have been the fine plaint of violins or the rustle of the silver wheat under the moon.

They pulled up behind a handsome brougham whose passengers were disembarking at the door. A lady got out, then an elderly gentleman, then another young lady, beautiful as sin. Benjamin started; an almost chemical change seemed to dissolve and recompose the very elements of his body. A rigour passed over him, blood rose into his cheeks, his forehead, and there was a steady thumping in his ears. It was first love.

The girl was slender and frail, with hair that was ashen under the moon and honey-colored under the sputtering gas-lamps of the porch. Over her shoulders was thrown a Spanish mantilla of softest yellow, butterflied in black; her feet were glittering buttons at the hem of her bustled dress.

Roger Button leaned over to his son. "That," he said, "is young Hildegarde Moncrief, the daughter of General Moncrief."

Benjamin nodded coldly. "Pretty little thing," he said indifferently. But when the boy had led the buggy away, he added: "Dad, you might introduce me to her."

They approached a group, of which Miss Moncrief was the centre. Reared in the old tradition, she curtsied low before Benjamin. Yes, he might have a dance. He thanked her and walked away—staggered away.

The interval until the time for his turn should arrive dragged itself out interminably. He stood close to the wall, silent, inscrutable, watching with murderous eyes the young bloods of Baltimore as they eddied around Hildegarde Moncrief, passionate admiration in their faces. How obnoxious they seemed to Benjamin; how intolerably rosy! Their curling brown whiskers aroused in him a feeling equivalent to indigestion.

But when his own time came, and he drifted with her out upon the changing floor to the music of the latest waltz from Paris, his jealousies and anxieties melted from him like a mantle of snow. Blind with enchantment, he felt that life was just beginning.

"You and your brother got here just as we did, didn't you?" asked Hildegarde, looking up at him with eyes that were like bright blue enamel.

Benjamin hesitated. If she took him for his father's brother, would it be best to enlighten her? He remembered his experience at Yale, so he decided against it. It would be rude to contradict a lady; it would be criminal to mar this exquisite occasion with the grotesque story of his origin. Later, perhaps. So he nodded, smiled, listened, was happy.

"I like men of your age," Hildegarde told him. "Young boys are so idiotic. They tell me how much champagne they drink at college, and how much money they lose playing cards. Men of your age know how to appreciate women."

Benjamin felt himself on the verge of a proposal—with an effort he choked back the impulse. "You're just the romantic age," she continued—"fifty. Twenty-five is too worldly wise; thirty is apt to be pale from overwork; forty is the age of long stories that take a whole cigar to tell; sixty is—oh, sixty is too near seventy; but fifty is the mellow age. I love fifty."

Fifty seemed to Benjamin a glorious age. He longed passionately to be fifty.

"I've always said," went on Hildegarde, "that I'd rather marry a man of fifty and be taken care of than many a man of thirty and take care of *him*."

For Benjamin the rest of the evening was bathed in a honey-colored mist. Hildegarde gave him two more dances, and they discovered that they were marvelously in accord on all the questions of the day. She was to go driving with him on the following Sunday, and then they would discuss all these questions further.

Going home in the phaeton just before the crack of dawn, when the first bees were humming and the fading moon glimmered in the cool dew, Benjamin knew vaguely that his father was discussing wholesale hardware.

"...And what do you think should merit our biggest attention after hammers and nails?" the elder Button was saying.

"Love," replied Benjamin absent-mindedly.

"Lugs?" exclaimed Roger Button, "Why, I've just covered the question of lugs."

Benjamin regarded him with dazed eyes just as the eastern sky was suddenly cracked with light, and an oriole yawned piercingly in the quickening trees...

When, six months later, the engagement of Miss Hildegarde Moncrief to Mr. Benjamin Button was made known (I say "made known," for General Moncrief declared he would rather fall upon his sword than announce it), the excitement in Baltimore society reached a feverish pitch. The almost forgotten story of Benjamin's birth was remembered and sent out upon the winds of scandal in picaresque and incredible forms. It was said that Benjamin was really the father of Roger Button, that he was his brother who had been in prison for forty years, that he was John Wilkes Booth in disguise—and, finally, that he had two small conical horns sprouting from his head.

The Sunday supplements of the New York papers played up the case with fascinating sketches which showed the head of Benjamin Button attached to a fish, to a snake, and, finally, to a body of solid brass. He became known, journalistically, as the Mystery Man of Maryland. But the true story, as is usually the case, had a very small circulation.

However, every one agreed with General Moncrief that it was "criminal" for a lovely girl who could have married any beau in Baltimore to throw herself into the arms of a man who was assuredly fifty. In vain Mr. Roger Button published his son's birth certificate in large type in the Baltimore *Blaze*. No one believed it. You had only to look at Benjamin and see.

On the part of the two people most concerned there was no wavering. So many of the stories about her fiancé were false that Hildegarde refused stubbornly to believe even the true one. In vain General Moncrief pointed out to her the high mortality among men of fifty—or, at least, among men who looked fifty; in vain he told her of the instability of the wholesale hardware business. Hildegarde had chosen to marry for mellowness, and marry she did....

In one particular, at least, the friends of Hildegarde Moncrief were mistaken. The wholesale hardware business prospered amazingly. In the fifteen years between Benjamin Button's marriage in 1880 and his father's retirement in 1895, the family fortune was doubled—and this was due largely to the younger member of the firm.

Needless to say, Baltimore eventually received the couple to its bosom. Even old General Moncrief became reconciled to his son-in-law when Benjamin gave him the money to bring out his *History of the Civil War* in twenty volumes, which had been refused by nine prominent publishers.

In Benjamin himself fifteen years had wrought many changes. It seemed to him that the blood flowed with new vigor through his veins. It began to be a pleasure to rise in the morning, to walk with an active step along the busy, sunny street, to work untiringly with his shipments of hammers and his cargoes of nails. It was in 1890 that he executed his famous business coup: he brought up the suggestion that *all nails used in nailing up the boxes in which nails are shipped are the property of the shippee*, a proposal which became a statute, was approved by Chief Justice Fossile, and saved Roger Button and Company, Wholesale Hardware, more than *six hundred nails every year*.

In addition, Benjamin discovered that he was becoming more and more attracted by the gay side of life. It was typical of his growing enthusiasm for pleasure that he was the first man in the city of Baltimore to own and run an automobile. Meeting him on the street, his contemporaries would stare enviously at the picture he made of health and vitality.

"He seems to grow younger every year," they would remark. And if old Roger Button, now sixty-five years old, had failed at first to give a proper welcome to his son he atoned at last by bestowing on him what amounted to adulation.

And here we come to an unpleasant subject that it will be well to pass over as quickly as possible. There was only one thing that worried Benjamin Button; his wife had ceased to attract him.

At that time Hildegarde was a woman of thirty-five, with a son, Roscoe, fourteen years old. In the early days of their marriage Benjamin had worshipped her. But, as the years passed, her honey-colored hair became an unexciting brown, the blue enamel of her eyes assumed the aspect of cheap crockery—moreover, and, most of all, she had become too settled in her ways, too placid, too content, too anemic in her excitements, and too sober in her taste. As a bride it had been she who had "dragged" Benjamin to dances and dinners—now conditions were reversed. She went out socially with him, but without enthusiasm, devoured already by that eternal inertia which comes to live with each of us one day and stays with us to the end.

Benjamin's discontent waxed stronger. At the outbreak of the Spanish-American War in 1898 his home had for him so little charm that he decided to join the army. With his business influence he obtained a commission as captain, and proved so adaptable to the work that he was made a major, and finally a lieutenant colonel just in time to participate in the celebrated charge up San Juan Hill. He was slightly wounded, and received a medal.

Benjamin had become so attached to the activity and excitement of array life that he regretted to give it up, but his business required attention, so he resigned his commission and came home. He was met at the station by a brass band and escorted to his house.

Hildegarde, waving a large silk flag, greeted him on the porch, and even as he kissed her he felt with a sinking of the heart that these three years had taken their toll. She was a woman of forty now, with a faint skirmish line of gray hairs in her head. The sight depressed him.

Up in his room he saw his reflection in the familiar mirror—he went closer and examined his own face with anxiety, comparing it after a moment with a photograph of himself in uniform taken just before the war.

"Good Lord!" he said aloud. The process was continuing. There was no doubt of it—he looked now like a man of thirty. Instead of being delighted, he was uneasy—he was growing younger. He had hitherto hoped that once he reached a bodily age equivalent to his age in years, the grotesque phenomenon which had marked his birth would cease to function. He shuddered. His destiny seemed to him awful, incredible.

When he came downstairs Hildegarde was waiting for him. She appeared annoyed, and he wondered if she had at last discovered that there was something amiss. It was with an effort to relieve the tension between them that he broached the matter at dinner in what he considered a delicate way.

"Well," he remarked lightly, "everybody says I look younger than ever."

Hildegarde regarded him with scorn. She sniffed. "Do you think it's anything to boast about?"

"I'm not boasting," he asserted uncomfortably. She sniffed again. "The idea," she said, and after a moment: "I should think you'd have enough pride to stop it."

"How can I?" he demanded.

"I'm not going to argue with you," she retorted. "But there's a right way of doing things and a wrong way. If you've made up your mind to be different from everybody else, I don't suppose I can stop you, but I really don't think it's very considerate."

"But, Hildegarde, I can't help it."

"You can too. You're simply stubborn. You think you don't want to be like any one else. You always have been that way, and you always will be. But just think how it would be if every one else looked at things as you do—what would the world be like?"

As this was an inane and unanswerable argument Benjamin made no reply, and from that time on a chasm began to widen between them. He wondered what possible fascination she had ever exercised over him.

To add to the breach, he found, as the new century gathered headway, that his thirst for gaiety grew stronger. Never a party of any kind in the city of Baltimore but he was there, dancing with the prettiest of the young married women, chatting with the most popular of the debutantes, and finding their company charming, while his wife, a dowager of evil omen, sat among the chaperons, now in haughty disapproval, and now following him with solemn, puzzled, and reproachful eyes.

"Look!" people would remark. "What a pity! A young fellow that age tied to a woman of forty-five. He must be twenty years younger than his wife." They had forgotten—as people inevitably forget—that back in 1880 their mammas and papas had also remarked about this same ill-matched pair.

Benjamin's growing unhappiness at home was compensated for by his many new interests. He took up golf and made a great success of it. He went in for dancing: in 1906 he was an expert at "The Boston," and in 1908 he was considered proficient at the "Maxine," while in 1909 his "Castle Walk" was the envy of every young man in town.

His social activities, of course, interfered to some extent with his business, but then he had worked hard at wholesale hardware for twenty-five years and felt that he could soon hand it on to his son, Roscoe, who had recently graduated from Harvard.

He and his son were, in fact, often mistaken for each other. This pleased Benjamin—he soon forgot the insidious fear that had come over him on his return from the Spanish-American War, and grew to take a naïve pleasure in his appearance. There was only one fly in the delicious ointment—he hated to appear in public with his wife. Hildegarde was almost fifty, and the sight of her made him feel absurd...

One September day in 1910—a few years after Roger Button & Co., Wholesale Hardware, had been handed over to young Roscoe Button—a man, apparently about twenty years old, entered himself as a freshman at Harvard University in Cambridge. He did not make the mistake of announcing that he would never see fifty again, nor did he mention the fact that his son had been graduated from the same institution ten years before.

He was admitted, and almost immediately attained a prominent position in the class, partly because he seemed a little older than the other freshmen, whose average age was about eighteen.

But his success was largely due to the fact that in the football game with Yale he played so brilliantly, with so much dash and with such a cold, remorseless anger that he scored seven touchdowns and fourteen field goals for Harvard, and caused one entire eleven of Yale men to be carried singly from the field, unconscious. He was the most celebrated man in college.

Strange to say, in his third or junior year he was scarcely able to "make" the team. The coaches said that he had lost weight, and it seemed to the more observant among them that he was not quite as tall as before. He made no touchdowns—indeed, he was retained on the team chiefly in hope that his enormous reputation would bring terror and disorganisation to the Yale team.

In his senior year he did not make the team at all. He had grown so slight and frail that one day he was taken by some sophomores for a freshman, an incident which humiliated him terribly. He became known as something of a prodigy—a senior who was surely no more than sixteen—and he was often shocked at the worldliness of some of his classmates. His studies seemed harder to him—he felt that they were too advanced. He had heard his classmates speak of St. Midas's, the famous preparatory school, at which so many of them had prepared for college, and he determined after his graduation to enter himself at St. Midas's, where the sheltered life among boys his own size would be more congenial to him.

Upon his graduation in 1914 he went home to Baltimore with his Harvard diploma in his pocket. Hildegarde was now residing in Italy, so Benjamin went to live with his son, Roscoe. But though he was welcomed in a general way there was obviously no heartiness in Roscoe's feeling toward him—there was even perceptible a tendency on his son's part to think that Benjamin, as he moped about the house in adolescent mooniness, was somewhat in the way. Roscoe was married now and prominent in Baltimore life, and he wanted no scandal to creep out in connection with his family.

Benjamin, no longer *persona grata* with the débutantes and younger college set, found himself left much done, except for the companionship of three or four fifteen-year-old boys in the neighborhood. His idea of going to St. Midas's school recurred to him.

"Say," he said to Roscoe one day, "I've told you over and over that I want to go to prep, school."

"Well, go, then," replied Roscoe shortly. The matter was distasteful to him, and he wished to avoid a discussion.

"I can't go alone," said Benjamin helplessly. "You'll have to enter me and take me up there."

"I haven't got time," declared Roscoe abruptly. His eyes narrowed and he looked uneasily at his father. "As a matter of fact," he added, "you'd better not go on with this business much longer. You better pull up short. You better—you better"—he paused and his face crimsoned as he sought for words—"you better turn right around and start back the other way. This has gone too far to be a joke. It isn't funny any longer. You—you behave yourself!"

Benjamin looked at him, on the verge of tears.

"And another thing," continued Roscoe, "when visitors are in the house I want you to call me 'Uncle'—not 'Roscoe,' but 'Uncle,' do you understand? It looks absurd for a boy of fifteen to call me by my first name. Perhaps you'd better call me 'Uncle' *all* the time, so you'll get used to it."

With a harsh look at his father, Roscoe turned away...

At the termination of this interview, Benjamin wandered dismally upstairs and stared at himself in the mirror. He had not shaved for three months, but he could find nothing on his face but a faint white down with which it seemed unnecessary to meddle. When he had first come home from Harvard, Roscoe had approached him with the proposition that he should wear eyeglasses and imitation whiskers glued to his cheeks, and it had seemed for a moment that the farce of his early years was to be repeated. But whiskers had itched and made him ashamed. He wept and Roscoe had reluctantly relented.

Benjamin opened a book of boys' stories, *The Boy Scouts in Bimini Bay*, and began to read. But he found himself thinking persistently about the war. America had joined the Allied cause during the preceding month, and Benjamin wanted to enlist, but, alas, sixteen was the minimum age, and he did not look that old. His true age, which was fifty-seven, would have disqualified him, anyway.

There was a knock at his door, and the butler appeared with a letter bearing a large official legend in the corner and addressed to Mr. Benjamin Button. Benjamin tore it open eagerly, and read the enclosure with delight. It informed him that many reserve officers who had served in the Spanish-American War were being called back into service with a higher rank, and it enclosed his commission as brigadier-general in the United States army with orders to report immediately.

Benjamin jumped to his feet fairly quivering with enthusiasm. This was what he had wanted. He seized his cap, and ten minutes later he had entered a large tailoring establishment on Charles Street, and asked in his uncertain treble to be measured for a uniform.

"Want to play soldier, sonny?" demanded a clerk casually.

Benjamin flushed. "Say! Never mind what I want!" he retorted angrily. "My name's Button and I live on Mt. Vernon Place, so you know I'm good for it."

"Well," admitted the clerk hesitantly, "if you're not, I guess your daddy is, all right."

Benjamin was measured, and a week later his uniform was completed. He had difficulty in obtaining the proper general's insignia because the dealer kept insisting to Benjamin that a nice V.W.C.A. badge would look just as well and be much more fun to play with.

Saying nothing to Roscoe, he left the house one night and proceeded by train to Camp Mosby, in South Carolina, where he was to command an infantry brigade. On a sultry April day he approached the entrance to the camp, paid off the taxicab which had brought him from the station, and turned to the sentry on guard.

"Get some one to handle my luggage!" he said briskly.

The sentry eyed him reproachfully. "Say," he remarked, "where you goin' with the general's duds, sonny?"

Benjamin, veteran of the Spanish-American War, whirled upon him with fire in his eye, but with, alas, a changing treble voice.

"Come to attention!" he tried to thunder; he paused for breath—then suddenly he saw the sentry snap his heels together and bring his rifle to the present. Benjamin concealed a smile of gratification, but when he glanced around his smile faded. It was not he who had inspired obedience, but an imposing artillery colonel who was approaching on horseback.

"Colonel!" called Benjamin shrilly.

The colonel came up, drew rein, and looked coolly down at him with a twinkle in his eyes. "Whose little boy are you?" he demanded kindly.

"I'll soon darn well show you whose little boy I am!" retorted Benjamin in a ferocious voice. "Get down off that horse!"

The colonel roared with laughter.

"You want him, eh, general?"

"Here!" cried Benjamin desperately. "Read this." And he thrust his commission toward the colonel.

The colonel read it, his eyes popping from their sockets.

"Where'd you get this?" he demanded, slipping the document into his own pocket.

"I got it from the Government, as you'll soon find out!"

"You come along with me," said the colonel with a peculiar look. "We'll go up to headquarters and talk this over. Come along."

The colonel turned and began walking his horse in the direction of headquarters. There was nothing for Benjamin to do but follow with as much dignity as possible—meanwhile promising himself a stern revenge.

But this revenge did not materialize. Two days later, however, his son Roscoe materialized from Baltimore, hot and cross from a hasty trip, and escorted the weeping general, *sans* uniform, back to his home.

II

In 1920 Roscoe Button's first child was born. During the attendant festivities, however, no one thought it "the thing" to mention, that the little grubby boy, apparently about ten years of age who played around the house with lead soldiers and a miniature circus, was the new baby's own grandfather.

No one disliked the little boy whose fresh, cheerful face was crossed with just a hint of sadness, but to Roscoe Button his presence was a source of torment. In the idiom of his generation Roscoe did not consider the matter "efficient." It seemed to him that his father, in refusing to look sixty, had not behaved like a "red-blooded he-man"—this was Roscoe's favorite expression—but in a curious and perverse manner. Indeed, to think about the matter for as much as a half an hour drove him to the edge of insanity. Roscoe believed that "live wires" should keep young, but carrying it out on such a scale was—was—was inefficient. And there Roscoe rested.

Five years later Roscoe's little boy had grown old enough to play childish games with little Benjamin under the supervision of the same nurse. Roscoe took them both to kindergarten on the same day, and Benjamin found that playing with little strips of colored paper, making mats and chains and curious and beautiful designs, was the most fascinating game in the world. Once he was bad and had to stand in the corner—then he cried—but for the most part there were gay hours in the cheerful room, with the sunlight coming in the windows and Miss Bailey's kind hand resting for a moment now and then in his tousled hair.

Roscoe's son moved up into the first grade after a year, but Benjamin stayed on in the kindergarten. He was very happy. Sometimes when other tots talked about what they would do when they grew up a shadow would cross his little face as if in a dim, childish way he realized that those were things in which he was never to share.

The days flowed on in monotonous content. He went back a third year to the kindergarten, but he was too little now to understand what the bright shining strips of paper were for. He cried because the other boys were bigger than he, and he was afraid of them. The teacher talked to him, but though he tried to understand he could not understand at all.

He was taken from the kindergarten. His nurse, Nana, in her starched gingham dress, became the centre of his tiny world. On bright days they walked in the park; Nana would point at a great gray monster and say "elephant," and Benjamin would say it after her, and when he was being undressed for bed that night he would say it over and over aloud to her: "Elyphant, elyphant, elyphant." Sometimes Nana let him jump on the bed, which was fun, because if you sat down exactly right it would bounce you up on your feet again, and if you said "Ah" for a long time while you jumped you got a very pleasing broken vocal effect.

He loved to take a big cane from the hat-rack and go around hitting chairs and tables with it and saying: "Fight, fight, fight." When there were people there the old ladies would cluck at him, which interested him, and the young ladies would try to kiss him, which he submitted to with mild boredom. And when the long day was done at five o'clock he would go upstairs with Nana and be fed on oatmeal and nice soft mushy foods with a spoon.

There were no troublesome memories in his childish sleep; no token came to him of his brave days at college, of the glittering years when he flustered the hearts of many girls. There were only the white, safe walls of his crib and Nana and a man who came to see him sometimes, and a great big orange ball that Nana pointed at just before his twilight bed hour and called "sun." When the sun went his eyes were sleepy—there were no dreams, no dreams to haunt him.

The past—the wild charge at the head of his men up San Juan Hill; the first years of his marriage when he worked late into the summer dusk down in the busy city for young Hildegarde whom he loved; the days before that when he sat smoking far into the night in the gloomy old Button house on Monroe Street with his grandfather-all these had faded like unsubstantial dreams from his mind as though they had never been. He did not remember.

He did not remember clearly whether the milk was warm or cool at his last feeding or how the days passed—there was only his crib and Nana's familiar presence. And then he remembered nothing. When he was hungry he cried—that was all. Through the noons and nights he breathed and over him there were soft mumblings and murmurings that he scarcely heard, and faintly differentiated smells, and light and darkness.

Then it was all dark, and his white crib and the dim faces that moved above him, and the warm sweet aroma of the milk, faded out altogether from his mind.

O RUSSET WITCH!

Merlin Grainger was employed by the Moonlight Quill Bookshop, which you may have visited, just around the corner from the Ritz-Carlton on Forty-Seventh Street. The Moonlight Quill is, or rather was, a very romantic little store, considered radical and admitted dark. It was spotted interiorly with red and orange posters of breathless exotic intent, and lit no less by the shiny reflecting bindings of special editions than by the great squat lamp of crimson satin that, lighted through all the day, swung overhead. It was truly a mellow bookshop. The words "Moonlight Quill" were worked over the door in a sort of serpentine embroidery. The windows seemed always full of something that had passed the literary censors with little to spare; volumes with covers of deep orange that offer their titles on little white paper squares. And over all there was the smell of the musk, which the clever, inscrutable Mr. Moonlight Quill ordered to be sprinkled about-the smell half of a curiosity shop in Dickens' London and half of a coffeehouse on the warm shores of the Bosphorus.

From nine until five-thirty Merlin Grainger asked bored old ladies in black and young men with dark circles under their eyes if they "cared for this fellow" or were interested in first editions. Did they buy novels with Arabs on the cover, or books that gave Shakespeare's newest sonnets as dictated psychically to Miss Sutton of South Dakota? he sniffed. As a matter of fact, his own taste ran to these latter, but as an employee at the Moonlight Quill he assumed for the working day the attitude of a disillusioned connoisseur.

After he had crawled over the window display to pull down the front shade at five-thirty every afternoon, and said goodbye to the mysterious Mr. Moonlight Quill and the lady clerk, Miss McCracken, and the lady stenographer, Miss Masters, he went home to the girl, Caroline. He did not eat supper with Caroline. It is unbelievable that Caroline would have considered eating off his bureau with the collar buttons dangerously near the cottage cheese, and the ends of Merlin's necktie just missing his glass of milk—he had never asked her to eat with him. He ate alone. He went into Braegdort's delicatessen on Sixth Avenue and bought a box of crackers, a tube of anchovy paste, and some oranges, or else a little jar of sausages and some potato salad and a bottled soft drink, and with these in a brown package he went to his room at Fifty-something

West Fifty-Eighth Street and ate his supper and saw Caroline.

Caroline was a very young and gay person who lived with some older lady and was possibly nineteen. She was like a ghost in that she never existed until evening. She sprang into life when the lights went on in her apartment at about six, and she disappeared, at the latest, about midnight. Her apartment was a nice one, in a nice building with a white stone front, opposite the south side of Central Park. The back of her apartment faced the single window of the single room occupied by the single Mr. Grainger.

He called her Caroline because there was a picture that looked like her on the jacket of a book of that name down at the Moonlight Quill.

Now, Merlin Grainger was a thin young man of twenty-five, with dark hair and no mustache or beard or anything like that, but Caroline was dazzling and light, with a shimmering morass of russet waves to take the place of hair, and the sort of features that remind you of kisses—the sort of features you thought belonged to your first love, but know, when you come across an old picture, didn't. She dressed in pink or blue usually, but of late she had sometimes put on a slender black gown that was evidently her especial pride, for whenever she wore it she would stand regarding a certain place on the wall, which Merlin thought most be a mirror. She sat usually in the profile chair near the window, but sometimes honored the *chaise longue* by the lamp, and often she leaned 'way back and smoked a cigarette with posturings of her arms and hands that Merlin considered very graceful.

At another time she had come to the window and stood in it magnificently, and looked out because the moon had lost its way and was dripping the strangest and most transforming brilliance into the areaway between, turning the motif of ash cans and clotheslines into a vivid impressionism of silver casks and gigantic gossamer cobwebs. Merlin was sitting in plain sight, eating cottage cheese with sugar and milk on it; and so quickly did he reach out for the window cord that he tipped the cottage cheese into his lap with his free hand—and the milk was cold and the sugar made spots on his trousers, and he was sure that she had seen him after all.

Sometimes there were callers—men in dinner coats, who stood and bowed, hat in hand and coat on arm, as they talked to Caroline; then bowed some more and followed her out of the light, obviously bound for a play or for a dance. Other young men came and sat and smoked cigarettes, and seemed trying to tell Caroline something—

she sitting either in the profile chair and watching them with eager intentness or else in the chaise longue by the lamp, looking very lovely and youthfully inscrutable indeed.

Merlin enjoyed these calls. Of some of the men he approved. Others won only his grudging toleration, one or two he loathed—especially the most frequent caller, a man with black hair and a black goatee and a pitch-dark soul, who seemed to Merlin vaguely familiar, but whom he was never quite able to recognize.

Now, Merlin's whole life was not "bound up with this romance he had constructed"; it was not "the happiest hour of his day." He never arrived in time to rescue Caroline from "clutches"; nor did he even marry her. A much stranger thing happened than any of these, and it is this strange thing that will presently be set down here. It began one October afternoon when she walked briskly into the mellow interior of the Moonlight Quill.

It was a dark afternoon, threatening rain and the end of the world, and done in that particularly gloomy gray in which only New York afternoons indulge. A breeze was crying down the streets, whisking along battered newspapers and pieces of things, and little lights were pricking out all the windows—it was so desolate that one was sorry for the tops of sky-scrapers lost up there in the dark green and gray heaven, and felt that now surely the farce was to close, and presently all the buildings would collapse like card houses, and pile up in a dusty, sardonic heap upon all the millions who presumed to wind in and out of them.

At least these were the sort of musings that lay heavily upon the soul of Merlin Grainger, as he stood by the window putting a dozen books back in a row after a cyclonic visit by a lady with ermine trimmings. He looked out of the window full of the most distressing thoughts—of the early novels of H. G. Wells, of the boot of Genesis, of how Thomas Edison had said that in thirty years there would be no dwelling-houses upon the island, but only a vast and turbulent bazaar; and then he set the last book right side up, turned—and Caroline walked coolly into the shop.

She was dressed in a jaunty but conventional walking costume—he remembered this when he thought about it later. Her skirt was plaid, pleated like a concertina; her jacket was a soft but brisk tan; her shoes and spats were brown and her hat, small and trim, completed her like the top of a very expensive and beautifully filled candy box.

Merlin, breathless and startled, advanced nervously toward her.

"Good afternoon—" he said, and then stopped—why, he did not know, except that it came to him that something very portentous in his life was about to occur, and that it would need no furbishing but silence, and the proper amount of expectant attention. And in that minute before the thing began to happen he had the sense of a breathless second hanging suspended in time: he saw through the glass partition that bounded off the little office the malevolent conical head of his employer, Mr. Moonlight Quill, bent over his correspondence. He saw Miss McCracken and Miss Masters as two patches of hair drooping over piles of paper; he saw the crimson lamp overhead, and noticed with a touch of pleasure how really pleasant and romantic it made the bookstore seem.

Then the thing happened, or rather it began to happen. Caroline picked up a volume of poems lying loose upon a pile, fingered it absently with her slender white hand, and suddenly, with an easy gesture, tossed it upward toward the ceiling where it disappeared in the crimson lamp and lodged there, seen through the illuminated silk as a dark, bulging rectangle. This pleased her—she broke into young, contagious laughter, in which Merlin found himself presently joining.

"It stayed up!" she cried merrily. "It stayed up, didn't it?" To both of them this seemed the height of brilliant absurdity. Their laughter mingled, filled the bookshop, and Merlin was glad to find that her voice was rich and full of sorcery.

"Try another," he found himself suggesting— "try a red one."

At this her laughter increased, and she had to rest her hands upon the stack to steady herself.

"Try another," she managed to articulate between spasms of mirth. "Oh, golly, try another!"

"Try two."

"Yes, try two. Oh, I'll choke if I don't stop laughing. Here it goes."

Suiting her action to the word, she picked up a red book and sent it in a gentle hyperbola toward the ceiling, where it sank into the lamp beside the first. It was a few minutes before either of them could do more than rock back and forth in helpless glee; but then by mutual agreement they took up the sport anew, this time in unison. Merlin seized a large, specially bound French classic and whirled it upward. Applauding his own accuracy, he took a bestseller in one hand and a book on barnacles in the other, and waited breathlessly while she made her shot. Then the business waxed fast and furious—sometimes they alternated, and, watching, he found how supple she was in every movement; sometimes one of them made shot after shot, picking up the nearest book, sending it off, merely taking time to follow it with a glance before reaching for another. Within three minutes they had cleared a little place on the table, and the lamp of crimson satin was so bulging with books that it was near breaking.

"Silly game, basketball," she cried scornfully as a book left her hand. "High school girls play it in hideous bloomers."

"Idiotic," he agreed.

She paused in the act of tossing a book, and replaced it suddenly in its position on the table.

"I think we've got room to sit down now," she said gravely.

They had; they had cleared an ample space for two. With a faint touch of nervousness Merlin glanced toward Mr. Moonlight Quill's glass partition, but the three heads were still bent earnestly over their work, and it was evident that they had not seen what had gone on in the shop. So when Caroline put her hands on the table and hoisted herself up Merlin calmly imitated her, and they sat side-by-side looking very earnestly at each other.

"I had to see you," she began, with a rather pathetic expression in her brown eyes.

"I know."

"It was that last time," she continued, her voice trembling a little, though she tried to keep it steady. "I was frightened. I don't like you to eat off the dresser. I'm so afraid you'll—you'll swallow a collar button."

"I did once—almost," he confessed reluctantly, "but it's not so easy, you know. I mean you can swallow the flat part easy enough or else the other part—that is, separately—but for a whole collar button you'd have to have a specially made throat." He was astonishing himself by the debonair appropriateness of his remarks. Words seemed for the first time in his life to ran at him shrieking to be used, gathering themselves into carefully arranged squads and platoons, and being presented to him by punctilious adjutants of paragraphs.

"That's what scared me," she said. "I knew you had to have a specially made throat—and I knew, at least I felt sure, that you didn't have one."

He nodded frankly.

"I haven't. It costs money to have one—more money unfortunately than I possess."

He felt no shame in saying this—rather a delight in making the admission—he knew that nothing he could say or do would be beyond her comprehension; least of all his poverty, and the
86

practical impossibility of ever extricating himself from it.

Caroline looked down at her wristwatch, and with a little cry slid from the table to her feet.

"It's after five," she cried. "I didn't realize. I have to be at the Ritz at five-thirty. Let's hurry and get this done. I've got a bet on it."

With one accord they set to work. Caroline began the matter by seizing a book on insects and sending it whizzing, and finally crashing through the glass partition that housed Mr. Moonlight Quill. The proprietor glanced up with a wild look, brushed a few pieces of glass from his desk, and went on with his letters. Miss McCracken gave no sign of having heard—only Miss Masters started and gave a little frightened scream before she bent to her task again.

But to Merlin and Caroline it didn't matter. In a perfect orgy of energy they were hurling book after book in all directions until sometimes three or four were in the air at once, smashing against shelves, cracking the glass of pictures on the walls, falling in bruised and torn heaps upon the floor. It was fortunate that no customers happened to come in, for it is certain they would never have come in again—the noise was too tremendous, a noise of smashing and ripping and tearing, mixed now and then with the tinkling of glass, the quick breathing of the two throwers, and the intermittent outbursts of laughter to which both of them periodically surrendered.

At five-thirty Caroline tossed a last book at the lamp, and gave the final impetus to the load it carried. The weakened silk tore and dropped its cargo in one vast splattering of white and color to the already littered floor. Then with a sigh of relief she turned to Merlin and held out her hand.

"Goodbye," she said simply.

"Are you going?" He knew she was. His question was simply a lingering wile to detain her and extract for another moment that dazzling essence of light he drew from her presence, to continue his enormous satisfaction in her features, which were like kisses and, he thought, like the features of a girl he had known back in 1910. For a minute he pressed the softness of her hand—then she smiled and withdrew it and, before he could spring to open the door, she had done it herself and was gone out into the turbid and ominous twilight that brooded narrowly over Forty-seventh Street.

I would like to tell you how Merlin, having seen how beauty regards the wisdom of the years, walked into the little partition of Mr. Moonlight Quill and gave up his job then and there; thence issuing out into the street a much finer and nobler and increasingly ironic man. But the truth is much more commonplace. Merlin Grainger stood up and surveyed the wreck of the bookshop, the ruined volumes, the torn silk remnants of the once beautiful crimson lamp, the crystalline sprinkling of broken glass which lay in iridescent dust over the whole interior—and then he went to a corner where a broom was kept and began cleaning up and rearranging and, as far as he was able, restoring the shop to its former condition. He found that, though some few of the books were uninjured, most of them had suffered in varying extents. The backs were off some, the pages were torn from others, still others were just slightly cracked in the front, which, as all careless book returners know, makes a book unsalable, and therefore secondhand.

Nevertheless by six o'clock he had done much to repair the damage. He had returned the books to their original places, swept the floor, and put new lights in the sockets overhead. The red shade itself was ruined beyond redemption, and Merlin thought in some trepidation that the money to replace it might have to come out of his salary. At six, therefore, having done the best he could, he crawled over the front window display to pull down the blind. As he was treading delicately back, he saw Mr. Moonlight Quill rise from his desk, put on his overcoat and hat, and emerge into the shop. He nodded mysteriously at Merlin and went toward the door. With his hand on the knob he paused, turned around, and in a voice curiously compounded of ferocity and uncertainty, he said:

"If that girl comes in here again, you tell her to behave."

With that he opened the door, drowning Merlin's meek "Yessir" in its creak, and went out.

Merlin stood there for a moment, deciding wisely not to worry about what was for the present only a possible futurity, and then he went into the back of the shop and invited Miss Masters to have supper with him at Pulpat's French Restaurant, where one could still obtain red wine at dinner, despite the Great Federal Government. Miss Masters accepted.

"Wine makes me feel all tingly," she said.

Merlin laughed inwardly as he compared her to Caroline, or rather as he didn't compare her. There was no comparison.

II

Mr. Moonlight Quill, mysterious, exotic, and oriental in temperament was, nevertheless, a man of decision. And it was with decision that he approached the problem of his wrecked shop. Unless he should make an outlay equal to the original cost of his entire stock—a step which for certain private reasons he did not wish to take—it would be impossible for him to continue in business with the Moonlight Quill as before. There was but one thing to do. He promptly turned his establishment from an up-to-the-minute bookstore into a second-hand bookshop. The damaged books were marked down from twenty-five to fifty per cent, the name over the door whose serpentine embroidery had once shone so insolently bright, was allowed to grow dim and take on the indescribably vague color of old paint, and, having a strong penchant for ceremonial, the proprietor even went so far as to buy two skullcaps of shoddy red felt, one for himself and one for his clerk, Merlin Grainger. Moreover, he let his goatee grow until it resembled the tail-feathers of an ancient sparrow and substituted for a once dapper business suit a reverence-inspiring affair of shiny alpaca.

In fact, within a year after Caroline's catastrophic visit to the bookshop the only thing in it that preserved any semblance of being up to date was Miss Masters. Miss McCracken had followed in the footsteps of Mr. Moonlight Quill and become an intolerable dowd.

For Merlin too, from a feeling compounded of loyalty and listlessness, had let his exterior take on the semblance of a deserted garden. He accepted the red felt skullcap as a symbol of his decay. Always a young man known, as a "pusher," he had been, since the day of his graduation from the manual training department of a New York High School, an inveterate brusher of clothes, hair, teeth, and even eyebrows, and had learned the value of laying all his clean socks toe upon toe and heel upon heel in a certain drawer of his bureau, which would be known as the sock drawer.

These things, he felt, had won him his place in the greatest splendor of the Moonlight Quill. It was due to them that he was not still making "chests useful for keeping things," as he was taught with breathless practicality in High School, and selling them to whoever had use of such chests—possibly undertakers. Nevertheless when the progressive Moonlight Quill became the retrogressive Moonlight Quill he preferred to sink with it, and so took to letting his suits gather undisturbed the wispy burdens of the air and to throwing his socks indiscriminately into the shirt drawer, the underwear drawer, and even into no drawer at all. It was not uncommon in his new carelessness to let many of his clean clothes go directly back to the laundry without having ever been worn, a common eccentricity of impoverished bachelors.

And this in the face of his favorite magazines, which at that time were fairly staggering with articles by successful authors against the frightful impudence of the condemned poor, such as the buying of wearable shirts and nice cuts of meat, and the fact that they preferred good investments in personal jewelry to respectable ones in four per cent saving-banks.

It was indeed a strange state of affairs and a sorry one for many worthy and God-fearing men. For the first time in the history of the Republic almost anyone north of Georgia could change a one-dollar bill. But as at that time the cent was rapidly approaching the purchasing power of the Chinese ubu and was only a thing you got back occasionally after paying for a soft drink, and could use merely in getting your correct weight, this was perhaps not so strange a phenomenon as it at first seems. It was too curious a state of things, however, for Merlin Grainger to take the step that he did take—the hazardous, almost involuntary step of proposing to Miss Masters. Stranger still that she accepted him.

It was at Pulpat's on Saturday night and over a $1.75 bottle of water diluted with *vin ordinaire* that the proposal occurred.

"Wine makes me feel all tingly, doesn't it you?" chattered Miss Masters gaily.

"Yes," answered Merlin absently; and then, after a long and pregnant pause: "Miss Masters—Olive—I want to say something to you if you'll listen to me."

The tingliness of Miss Masters (who knew what was coming) increased until it seemed that she would shortly be electrocuted by her own nervous reactions. But her "Yes, Merlin," came without a sign or flicker of interior disturbance. Merlin swallowed a stray bit of air that he found in his mouth.

"I have no fortune," he said with the manner of making an announcement. "I have no fortune at all."

Their eyes met, locked, became wistful, and dreamy and beautiful.

"Olive," he told her, "I love you."

"I love you too, Merlin," she answered simply. "Shall we have another bottle of wine?"

"Yes," he cried, his heart beating at a great rate. "Do you mean—"

"To drink to our engagement," she interrupted bravely. "May it be a short one!"

"No!" he almost shouted, bringing his fist fiercely down upon the table. "May it last forever!"

"What?"

"I mean—oh, I see what you mean. You're right. May it be a short one." He laughed and added, "My error."

After the wine arrived they discussed the matter thoroughly.

"We'll have to take a small apartment at first," he said, "and I believe, yes, by golly, I know there's a small one in the house where I live, a big room and a sort of a dressing-room-kitchenette and the use of a bath on the same floor."

She clapped her hands happily, and he thought how pretty she was really, that is, the upper part of her face—from the bridge of the nose down she was somewhat out of true. She continued enthusiastically:

"And as soon as we can afford it we'll take a real swell apartment, with an elevator and a telephone girl."

"And after that a place in the country—and a car."

"I can't imagine nothing more fun. Can you?"

Merlin fell silent a moment. He was thinking that he would have to give up his room, the fourth floor rear. Yet it mattered very little now. During the past year and a half—in fact, from the very date of Caroline's visit to the Moonlight Quill—he had never seen her. For a week after that visit her lights had failed to go on—darkness brooded out into the areaway, seemed to grope blindly in at his expectant, uncurtained window. Then the lights had appeared at last, and instead of Caroline and her callers they stowed a stodgy family—a little man with a bristly mustache and a full-bosomed woman who spent her evenings patting her hips and rearranging bric-à-brac. After two days of them Merlin had callously pulled down his shade.

No, Merlin could think of nothing more fun than rising in the world with Olive. There would be a cottage in a suburb, a cottage painted blue, just one class below the sort of cottages that are of white stucco with a green roof. In the grass around the cottage would be rusty trowels and a broken green bench and a baby carriage with a wicker body that sagged to the left. And around the grass and the baby carriage and the cottage itself, around his whole world there would be the arms of Olive, a little stouter, the arms of her neo-Olivian period, when, as she walked, her cheeks would tremble up and down ever so slightly from too much face-massaging. He could hear her voice now, two spoons' length away:

"I knew you were going to say this tonight, Merlin. I could see—"

She could see. Ah—suddenly he wondered how much she could see. Could she see that the girl who had come in with a party of three men and sat down at the next table was Caroline? Ah, could she see that? Could she see that the men brought with them liquor far more potent than Pulpat's red ink condensed threefold...

Merlin stared breathlessly, half-hearing through an auditory ether Olive's low, soft monologue, as like a persistent honeybee she sucked sweetness from her memorable hour. Merlin was listening to the clinking of ice and the fine laughter of all four at some pleasantry—and that laughter of Caroline's that he knew so well stirred him, lifted him, called his heart imperiously over to her table, whither it obediently went. He could see her quite plainly, and he fancied that in the last year and a half she had changed, if ever so slightly. Was it the light or were her cheeks a little thinner and her eyes less fresh, if more liquid, than of old? Yet the shadows were still purple in her russet hair; her mouth hinted yet of kisses, as did the profile that came sometimes between his eyes and a row of books, when it was twilight in the book-shop where the crimson lamp presided no more.

And she had been drinking. The threefold flush in her cheeks was compounded of youth and wine and fine cosmetic—that he could tell. She was making great amusement for the young man on her left and the portly person on her right, and even for the old fellow opposite her, for the latter from time to time uttered the shocked and mildly reproachful cackles of another generation. Merlin caught the words of a song she was intermittently singing—

"Just snap your fingers at care, Don't cross the bridge 'til you're there—"

The portly person filled her glass with chill amber. A waiter after several trips about the table, and many helpless glances at Caroline, who was maintaining a cheerful, futile questionnaire as to the succulence of this dish or that, managed to obtain the semblance of an order and hurried away…

Olive was speaking to Merlin—

"When, then?" she asked, her voice faintly shaded with disappointment. He realized that he had just answered no to some question she had asked him.

"Oh, sometime."

"Don't you—care?"

A rather pathetic poignancy in her question brought his eyes back to her.

"As soon as possible, dear," he replied with surprising tenderness.

"In two months—in June."

"So soon?" Her delightful excitement quite took her breath away.

"Oh, yes, I think we'd better say June. No use waiting."

Olive began to pretend that two months was really too short a time for her to make preparations. Wasn't he a bad boy! Wasn't he impatient, though! Well, she'd show him he mustn't be too quick with *her*. Indeed he was so sudden she didn't exactly know whether she ought to marry him at all.

"June," he repeated sternly.

Olive sighed and smiled and drank her coffee, her little finger lifted high above the others in true refined fashion. A stray thought came to Merlin that he would like to buy five rings and throw at it.

"By gosh!" he exclaimed aloud. Soon he *would* be putting rings on one of her fingers.

His eyes swung sharply to the right. The party of four had become so riotous that the headwaiter had approached and spoken to them. Caroline was arguing with this headwaiter in a raised voice, a voice so clear and young that it seemed as though the whole restaurant would listen—the whole restaurant except Olive Masters, self-absorbed in her new secret.

"How do you do?" Caroline was saying. "Probably the handsomest head-waiter in captivity. Too much noise? Very unfortunate. Something'll have to be done about it. Gerald"—she addressed the man on her right—"the headwaiter says there's too much noise. Appeals to us to have it stopped. What'll I say?"

"Sh!" remonstrated Gerald, with laughter. "Sh!" and Merlin heard him add in an undertone: "All the bourgeoisie will be aroused. This is where the floorwalkers learn French."

Caroline sat up straight in sudden alertness.

"Where's a floorwalker?" she cried. "Show me a floorwalker." This seemed to amuse the party, for they all, including Caroline, burst into renewed laughter. The headwaiter, after a last conscientious but despairing admonition, became Gallic with his shoulders and retired into the background.

Pulpat's, as every one knows, has the unvarying respectability of the table d'hôte. It is not a gay place in the conventional sense. One comes, drinks the red wine, talks perhaps a little more and a little louder than usual under the low, smoky ceilings, and then goes home. It closes up at nine-thirty, tight as a drum; the policeman is paid off and given an extra bottle of wine for the missis, the coatroom girl hands her tips to the col-

100

lector, and then darkness crushes the little round tables out of sight and life. But excitement was prepared for Pulpat's this evening—excitement of no mean variety. A girl with russet, purple-shadowed hair mounted to her tabletop and began to dance thereon.

"*Sacré nom de Dieu!* Come down off there!" cried the headwaiter. "Stop that music!"

But the musicians were already playing so loud that they could pretend not to hear his order; having once been young, they played louder and gayer than ever, and Caroline danced with grace and vivacity, her pink, filmy dress swirling about her, her agile arms playing in supple, tenuous gestures along the smoky air.

A group of Frenchmen at a table near by broke into cries of applause, in which other parties joined—in a moment the room was full of clapping and shouting; half the diners were on their feet, crowding up, and on the outskirts the hastily summoned proprietor was giving indistinct vocal evidences of his desire to put an end to this thing as quickly as possible.

"...Merlin!" cried Olive, awake, aroused at last; "she's such a wicked girl! Let's get out—now!"

The fascinated Merlin protested feebly that the check was not paid.

"It's all right. Lay five dollars on the table. I despise that girl. I can't *bear* to look at her." She was on her feet now, tagging at Merlin's arm.

Helplessly, listlessly, and then with what amounted to downright unwillingness, Merlin rose, followed Olive dumbly as she picked her way through the delirious clamor, now approaching its height and threatening to become a wild and memorable riot. Submissively he took his coat and stumbled up half a dozen steps into the moist April air outside, his ears still ringing with the sound of light feet on the table and of laughter all about and over the little world of the cafe. In silence they walked along toward Fifth Avenue and a bus.

It was not until next day that she told him about the wedding—how she had moved the date forward: it was much better that they should be married on the first of May.

III

And married they were, in a somewhat stuffy manner, under the chandelier of the flat where Olive lived with her mother. After marriage came elation, and then, gradually, the growth of weariness. Responsibility descended upon Merlin, the responsibility of making his thirty dollars a week and her twenty suffice to keep them respectably fat and to hide with decent garments the evidence that they were.

It was decided after several weeks of disastrous and well-nigh humiliating experiments with restaurants that they would join the great army of the delicatessen-fed, so he took up his old way of life again, in that he stopped every evening at Braegdort's delicatessen and bought potatoes in salad, ham in slices, and sometimes even stuffed tomatoes in bursts of extravagance.

Then he would trudge homeward, enter the dark hallway, and climb three rickety flights of stairs covered by an ancient carpet of long obliterated design. The hall had an ancient smell—of the vegetables of 1880, of the furniture polish in vogue when "Adam-and Eve" Bryan ran against William McKinley, of portieres an ounce heavier with dust, from worn-out shoes, and lint from dresses turned long since into patch-work quilts. This smell would pursue him up the stairs, revivified and made poignant at each landing by the aura of contemporary cooking, then, as he began the next flight, diminishing into the odor of the dead routine of dead generations.

Eventually would occur the door of his room, which slipped open with indecent willingness and closed with almost a sniff upon his "Hello, dear! Got a treat for you tonight."

Olive, who always rode home on the bus to "get a morsel of air," would be making the bed and hanging up things. At his call she would come up to him and give him a quick kiss with wide-open eyes, while he held her upright like a ladder, his hands on her two arms, as though she were a thing without equilibrium, and would, once he relinquished hold, fall stiffly backward to the floor. This is the kiss that comes in with the second year of marriage, succeeding the bride-groom kiss (which is rather stagey at best, say those who know about such things, and apt to be copied from passionate movies).

Then came supper, and after that they went out for a walk, up two blocks and through Central Park, or sometimes to a moving picture, which taught them patiently that they were the sort of people for whom life was ordered, and that something very grand and brave and beautiful would soon happen to them if they were docile and obedient to their rightful superiors and kept away from pleasure.

Such was their day for three years. Then change came into their lives: Olive had a baby, and as a result Merlin had a new influx of material resources. In the third week of Olive's confinement, after an hour of nervous rehearsing, he went into the office of Mr. Moonlight Quill and demanded an enormous increase in salary.

"I've been here ten years," he said; "since I was nineteen. I've always tried to do my best in the interests of the business."

Mr. Moonlight Quill said that he would think it over. Next morning he announced, to Merlin's great delight, that he was going to put into effect a project long premeditated—he was going to retire from active work in the bookshop, confining himself to periodic visits and leaving Merlin as manager with a salary of fifty dollars a week and a one-tenth interest in the business. When the old man finished, Merlin's cheeks were glowing and his eyes full of tears. He seized his employer's hand and shook it violently, saying over and over again:

"It's very nice of you, sir. It's very white of you. It's very, very nice of you."

So after ten years of faithful work in the store he had won out at last. Looking back, he saw his own progress toward this hill of elation no longer as a sometimes sordid and always gray decade of worry and failing enthusiasm and failing dreams, years when the moonlight had grown duller in the areaway and the youth had faded out of Olive's face, but as a glorious and triumphant climb over obstacles which he had determinedly surmounted by unconquerable willpower. The optimistic self-delusion that had kept him from misery was seen now in the golden garments of stern resolution. Half a dozen times he had taken steps to leave the Moonlight Quill and soar upward, but through sheer faintheartedness he had stayed on. Strangely enough he now thought that those were times when he had exerted tremendous persistence and had "determined" to fight it out where he was.

At any rate, let us not for this moment begrudge Merlin his new and magnificent view of himself. He had arrived. At thirty he had reached a post of importance. He left the shop that evening fairly radiant, invested every penny in his pocket in the most tremendous feast that Braegdort's delicatessen offered, and staggered homeward with the great news and four gigantic paper bags. The fact that Olive was too sick to eat, that he made himself faintly but unmistakably ill by a struggle with four stuffed tomatoes, and that most of the food deteriorated rapidly in an iceless icebox: all next day did not mar the occasion. For the first time since the week of his marriage Merlin Grainger lived under a sky of unclouded tranquility.

The baby boy was christened Arthur, and life became dignified, significant, and, at length, centered. Merlin and Olive resigned themselves to a somewhat secondary place in their own cosmos; but what they lost in personality they regained in a sort of primordial pride. The country house did not come, but a month in an Asbury Park boardinghouse each summer filled the gap; and during Merlin's two weeks' holiday this excursion assumed the air of a really merry jaunt—especially when, with the baby asleep in a wide room opening technically on the sea, Merlin strolled with Olive along the thronged board-walk puffing at his cigar and trying to look like twenty thousand a year.

With some alarm at the slowing up of the days and the accelerating of the years, Merlin became thirty-one, thirty-two—then almost with a rush arrived at that age which, with all its washing and panning, can only muster a bare handful of the precious stuff of youth: he became thirty-five. And one day on Fifth Avenue he saw Caroline.

It was Sunday, a radiant, flowerful Easter morning and the avenue was a pageant of lilies and cutaways and happy April-colored bonnets. Twelve o'clock: the great churches were letting out their people—St. Simon's, St. Hilda's, the Church of the Epistles, opened their doors like wide mouths until the people pouring forth surely resembled happy laughter as they met and strolled and chattered, or else waved white bouquets at waiting chauffeurs.

In front of the Church of the Epistles stood its twelve vestrymen, carrying out the time-honored custom of giving away Easter eggs full of face powder to the church-going debutantes of the year. Around them delightedly danced the two thousand miraculously groomed children of the very rich, correctly cute and curled, shining like sparkling little jewels upon their mothers' fingers. Speaks the sentimentalist for the children of the poor? Ah, but the children of the rich, laundered, sweet smelling, complexioned of the country, and, above all, with soft, in-door voices.

Little Arthur was five, child of the middle class. Undistinguished, unnoticed, with a nose that forever marred what Grecian yearnings his features might have had, he held tightly to his mother's warm, sticky hand, and, with Merlin on his other side, moved, upon the home-coming throng. At Fifty-third Street, where there were two churches, the congestion was at its thickest, its richest. Their progress was of necessity retarded to such an extent that even little Arthur had not the slightest difficulty in keeping up. Then it was that Merlin perceived an open landaulet of deepest crimson, with handsome nickel trimmings, glide slowly up to the curb and come to a stop. In it sat Caroline.

She was dressed in black, a tight-fitting gown trimmed with lavender, flowered at the waist with a corsage of orchids. Merlin started and then gazed at her fearfully. For the first time in the eight years since his marriage he was encountering the girl again. But a girl no longer. Her figure was slim as ever—or perhaps not quite, for a certain boyish swagger, a sort of insolent adolescence, had gone the way of the first blooming of her cheeks. But she was beautiful; dignity was there now, and the charming lines of a fortuitous nine-and-twenty; and she sat in the car with such perfect appropriateness and self-possession that it made him breathless to watch her.

Suddenly she smiled—the smile of old, bright as that very Easter and its flowers, mellower than ever—yet somehow with not quite the radiance and infinite promise of that first smile back there in the bookshop nine years before. It was a steelier smile, disillusioned and sad.

But it was soft enough and smile enough to make a pair of young men in cutaway coats hurry over, to pull their high hats off their wetted, iridescent hair; to bring them, flustered and bowing, to the edge of her landaulet, where her lavender gloves gently touched their gray ones. And these two were presently joined by another, and then two more, until there was a rapidly swelling crowd around the landaulet. Merlin would hear a young man beside him say to his perhaps well-favored companion:

"If you'll just pardon me a moment, there's some one I *have* to speak to. Walk right ahead. I'll catch up."

Within three minutes every inch of the landaulet, front, back, and side, was occupied by a man—a man trying to construct a sentence clever enough to find its way to Caroline through the stream of conversation. Luckily for Merlin a portion of little Arthur's clothing had chosen the opportunity to threaten a collapse, and Olive had hurriedly rushed him over against a building for some extemporaneous repair work, so Merlin was able to watch, unhindered, the salon in the street.

The crowd swelled. A row formed in back of the first, two more behind that. In the midst, an orchid rising from a black bouquet, sat Caroline enthroned in her obliterated car, nodding and crying salutations and smiling with such true happiness that, of a sudden, a new relay of gentlemen had left their wives and consorts and were striding toward her.

The crowd, now phalanx deep, began to be augmented by the merely curious; men of all ages who could not possibly have known Caroline jostled over and melted into the circle of ever-increasing diameter, until the lady in lavender was the centre of a vast impromptu auditorium.

All about her were faces—clean-shaven, be-whiskered, old, young, ageless, and now, here and there, a woman. The mass was rapidly spreading to the opposite curb, and, as St. Anthony's around the corner let out its box-holders, it overflowed to the sidewalk and crushed up against the iron picket fence of a millionaire across the street. The motors speeding along the avenue were compelled to stop, and in a jiffy were piled three, five, and six deep at the edge of the crowd; auto-busses, top-heavy turtles of traffic, plunged into the jam, their passengers crowding to the edges of the roofs in wild excitement and peering down into the centre of the mass, which presently could hardly be seen from the mass's edge.

The crush had become terrific. No fashionable audience at a Yale-Princeton football game, no damp mob at a world's series, could be compared with the panoply that talked, stared, laughed, and honked about the lady in black and lavender. It was stupendous; it was terrible. A quarter mile down the block a half-frantic policeman called his precinct; on the same corner a frightened civilian crashed in the glass of a fire-alarm and sent in a wild paean for all the fire-engines of the city; up in an apartment high in one of the tall buildings a hysterical old maid telephoned in turn for the prohibition enforcement agent; the special deputies on Bolshevism, and the maternity ward of Bellevue Hospital.

The noise increased. The first fire engine arrived, filling the Sunday air with smoke, clanging and crying a brazen, metallic message down the high, resounding walls. In the notion that some terrible calamity had overtaken the city, two excited deacons ordered special services immediately and set tolling the great bells of St. Hilda's and St. Anthony's, presently joined by the jealous gongs of St. Simon's and the Church of the Epistles. Even far off in the Hudson and the East River the sounds of the commotion were heard, and the ferry-boats and tugs and ocean liners set up sirens and whistles that sailed in melancholy cadence, now varied, now reiterated, across the whole diagonal width of the city from Riverside Drive to the gray water-fronts of the lower East Side...

In the centre of her landaulet sat the lady in black and lavender, chatting pleasantly first with one, then with another of that fortunate few in cutaways who had found their way to speaking distance in the first rush. After a while she glanced around her and beside her with a look of growing annoyance.

She yawned and asked the man nearest her if he couldn't run in somewhere and get her a glass of water. The man apologized in some embarrassment. He could not have moved hand or foot. He could not have scratched his own ear...

As the first blast of the river sirens keened along the air, Olive fastened the last safety pin in little Arthur's rompers and looked up. Merlin saw her start, stiffen slowly like hardening stucco, and then give a little gasp of surprise and disapproval.

"That woman," she cried suddenly. "Oh!"

She flashed a glance at Merlin that mingled reproach and pain, and without another word gathered up little Arthur with one hand, grasped her husband by the other, and darted amazingly in a winding, bumping canter through the crowd. Somehow people gave way before her; somehow she managed to-retain her grasp on her son and husband; somehow she managed to emerge two blocks up, battered and disheveled, into an open space, and, without slowing up her pace, darted down a side-street. Then at last, when uproar had died away into a dim and distant clamor, did she come to a walk and set little Arthur upon his feet.

"And on Sunday, too! Hasn't she disgraced herself enough?" This was her only comment. She said it to Arthur, as she seemed to address her remarks to Arthur throughout the remainder of the day. For some curious and esoteric reason she had never once looked at her husband during the entire retreat.

IV

The years between thirty-five and sixty-five revolve before the passive mind as one unexplained, confusing merry-go-round. True, they are a merry-go-round of ill-gaited and windbroken horses, painted first in pastel colors, then in dull grays and browns, but perplexing and intolerably dizzy the thing is, as never were the merry-go-rounds of childhood or adolescence; as never, surely, were the certain-coursed, dynamic roller coasters of youth. For most men and women these thirty years are taken up with a gradual withdrawal from life, a retreat first from a front with many shelters, those myriad amusements and curiosities of youth, to a line with less, when we peel down our ambitions to one ambition, our recreations to one recreation, our friends to a few to whom we are anaesthetic; ending up at last in a solitary, desolate strong point that is not strong, where the shells now whistle abominably, now are but half-heard as, by turns frightened and tired, we sit waiting for death.

At forty, then, Merlin was no different from himself at thirty-five; a larger paunch, a gray twinkling near his ears, a more certain lack of vivacity in his walk. His forty-five differed from his forty by a like margin, unless one mention a slight deafness in his left ear. But at fifty-five the process had become a chemical change of immense rapidity. Yearly he was more and more an "old man" to his family—senile almost, so far as his wife was concerned. He was by this time complete owner of the bookshop. The mysterious Mr. Moonlight Quill, dead some five years and not survived by his wife, had deeded the whole stock and store to him, and there he still spent his days, conversant now by name with almost all that man has recorded for three thousand years, a human catalogue, an authority upon tooling and binding, upon folios and first editions, an accurate inventory of a thousand authors whom he could never have understood and had certainly never read.

At sixty-five he distinctly doddered. He had assumed the melancholy habits of the aged so often portrayed by the second old man in standard Victorian comedies. He consumed vast warehouses of time searching for mislaid spectacles.

He "nagged" his wife and was nagged in turn. He told the same jokes three or four times a year at the family table, and gave his son weird, impossible directions as to his conduct in life. Mentally and materially he was so entirely different from the Merlin Grainger of twenty-five that it seemed incongruous that he should bear the same name.

He worked still In the bookshop with the assistance of a youth, whom, of course, he considered very idle, indeed, and a new young woman, Miss Gaffney. Miss McCracken, ancient and unvenerable as himself, still kept the accounts. Young Arthur was gone into Wall Street to sell bonds, as all the young men seemed to be doing in that day. This, of course, was as it should be. Let old Merlin get what magic he could from his books—the place of young King Arthur was in the counting house.

One afternoon at four when he had slipped noiselessly up to the front of the store on his soft-soled slippers, led by a newly formed habit, of which, to be fair, he was rather ashamed, of spying upon the young man clerk, he looked casually out of the front window, straining his faded eyesight to reach the street. A limousine, large, portentous, impressive, had drawn to the curb, and the chauffeur, after dismounting and holding some sort of conversation with persons in the interior of the car, turned about and advanced in a bewildered fashion toward the entrance of the Moonlight Quill. He opened the door, shuffled in, and, glancing uncertainly at the old man in the skullcap, addressed him in a thick, murky voice, as though his words came through a fog.

"Do you—do you sell additions?"

Merlin nodded.

"The arithmetic books are in the back of the store."

The chauffeur took off his cap and scratched a close-cropped, fuzzy head.

"Oh, naw. This I want's a detecatif story." He jerked a thumb back toward the limousine. "She seen it in the paper. Firs' addition."

Merlin's interest quickened. Here was possibly a big sale.

"Oh, editions. Yes, we've advertised some firsts, but-detective stories, I-don't-believe-What was the title?"

"I forget. About a crime."

"About a crime. I have-well, I have 'The Crimes of the Borgias'-full morocco, London 1769, beautifully—"

"Naw," interrupted the chauffeur, "this was one fella did this crime. She seen you had it for sale in the paper." He rejected several possible titles with the air of connoisseur.

"'Silver Bones,'" he announced suddenly out of a slight pause.

"What?" demanded Merlin, suspecting that the stiffness of his sinews were being commented on.

"Silver Bones. That was the guy that done the crime."

"Silver Bones?"

"Silver Bones. Indian, maybe."

Merlin, stroked his grizzly cheeks. "Gees, Mister," went on the prospective purchaser, "if you wanna save me an awful bawln' out jes' try an' think. The old lady goes wile if everything don't run smooth."

But Merlin's musings on the subject of Silver Bones were as futile as his obliging search through the shelves, and five minutes later a very dejected charioteer wound his way back to his mistress. Through the glass Merlin could see the visible symbols of a tremendous uproar going on in the interior of the limousine. The chauffeur made wild, appealing gestures of his innocence, evidently to no avail, for when he turned around and climbed back into the driver's seat his expression was not a little dejected.

Then the door of the limousine opened and gave forth a pale and slender young man of about twenty, dressed in the attenuation of fashion and carrying a wisp of a cane. He entered the shop, walked past Merlin, and proceeded to take out a cigarette and light it. Merlin approached him.

"Anything I can do for you, sir?"

"Old boy," said the youth coolly, "there are several things; You can first let me smoke my ciggy in here out of sight of that old lady in the limousine, who happens to be my grandmother. Her knowledge as to whether I smoke it or not before my majority happens to be a matter of five thousand dollars to me. The second thing is that you should look up your first edition of the 'Crime of Sylvester Bonnard' that you advertised in last Sunday's *Times*. My grandmother there happens to want to take it off your hands."

Detecatif story! Crime of somebody! Silver Bones! All was explained. With a faint deprecatory chuckle, as if to say that he would have enjoyed this had life put him in the habit of enjoying anything, Merlin doddered away to the back of his shop where his treasures were kept, to get this latest investment which he had picked up rather cheaply at the sale of a big collection.

When he returned with it the young man was drawing on his cigarette and blowing out quantities of smoke with immense satisfaction.

"My God!" he said, "She keeps me so close to her the entire day running idiotic errands that this happens to be my first puff in six hours. What's the world coming to, I ask you, when a feeble old lady in the milk-toast era can dictate to a man as to his personal vices. I happen to be unwilling to be so dictated to. Let's see the book."

Merlin passed it to him tenderly and the young man, after opening it with a carelessness that gave a momentary jump to the book-dealer's heart, ran through the pages with his thumb.

"No illustrations, eh?" he commented. "Well, old boy, what's it worth? Speak up! We're willing to give you a fair price, though why I don't know."

"One hundred dollars," said Merlin with a frown.

The young man gave a startled whistle.

"Whew! Come on. You're not dealing with somebody from the corn belt. I happen to be a city-bred man and my grandmother happens to be a city-bred woman, though I'll admit it'd take a special tax appropriation to keep her in repair. We'll give you twenty-five dollars, and let me tell you that's liberal. We've got books in our attic, up in our attic with my old playthings, that were written before the old boy that wrote this was born."

Merlin stiffened, expressing a rigid and meticulous horror.

"Did your grandmother give you twenty-five dollars to buy this with?"

"She did not. She gave me fifty, but she expects change. I know that old lady."

"You tell her," said Merlin with dignity, "that she has missed a very great bargain."

"Give you forty," urged the young man. "Come on now—be reasonable and don't try to hold us up—"

Merlin had wheeled around with the precious volume under his arm and was about to return it to its special drawer in his office when there was a sudden interruption. With unheard-of magnificence the front door burst rather than swung open, and admitted in the dark interior a regal apparition in black silk and fur that bore rapidly down upon him. The cigarette leaped from the fingers of the urban young man and he gave breath to an inadvertent "Damn!"—but it was upon Merlin that the entrance seemed to have the most remarkable and incongruous effect—so strong an effect that the greatest treasure of his shop slipped from his hand and joined the cigarette on the floor. Before him stood Caroline.

She was an old woman, an old woman remarkably preserved, unusually handsome, unusually erect, but still an old woman. Her hair was a soft, beautiful white, elaborately dressed

121

and jeweled; her face, faintly rouged à la grande dame, showed webs of wrinkles at the edges of her eyes and two deeper lines in the form of stanchions connected her nose with the corners of her mouth. Her eyes were dim, ill natured, and querulous.

But it was Caroline without a doubt: Caroline's features though in decay; Caroline's figure, if brittle and stiff in movement; Caroline's manner, unmistakably compounded of a delightful insolence and an enviable self assurance; and, most of all, Caroline's voice, broken and shaky, yet with a ring in it that still could and did make chauffeurs want to drive laundry wagons and cause cigarettes to fall from the fingers of urban grandsons.

She stood and sniffed. Her eyes found the cigarette upon the floor.

"What's that?" she cried. The words were not a question—they were an entire litany of suspicion, accusation, confirmation, and decision. She tarried over them scarcely an instant. "Stand up!" she said to her grandson, "stand up and blow that nicotine out of your lungs!"

The young man looked at her in trepidation.

"Blow!" she commanded.

He pursed his lips feebly and blew into the air.

"Blow!" she repeated, more peremptorily than before.

He blew again, helplessly, ridiculously.

"Do you realize," she went on briskly, "that you've forfeited five thousand dollars in five minutes?"

Merlin momentarily expected the young man to fall pleading upon his knees, but such is the nobility of human nature that he remained standing—even blew again into the air, partly from nervousness, partly, no doubt, with some vague hope of reingratiating himself.

"Young ass!" cried Caroline. "Once more, just once more and you leave college and go to work."

This threat had such an overwhelming effect upon the young man that he took on an even paler pallor than was natural to him. But Caroline was not through.

"Do you think I don't know what you and your brothers, yes, and your asinine father too, think of me? Well, I do. You think I'm senile. You think I'm soft. I'm not!" She struck herself with her-fist as though to prove that she was a mass of muscle and sinew. "And I'll have more brains left when you've got me laid out in the drawing-room some sunny day than you and the rest of them were born with."

"But Grandmother—"

"Be quiet. You, a thin little stick of a boy, who if it weren't for my money might have risen to be a journeyman barber out in the Bronx—Let me see your hands. Ugh! The hands of a barber—*you* presume to be smart with *me*, who once had three counts and a bona fide duke, not to mention half a dozen papal titles pursue me from the city of Rome to the city of New York." She paused, took breath. "Stand up! Blow'!"

The young man obediently blew. Simultaneously the door opened and an excited gentleman of middle age who wore a coat and hat trimmed with fur, and seemed, moreover, to be trimmed with the same sort of fur himself on upper lip and chin, rushed into the store and up to Caroline.

"Found you at last," he cried. "Been looking for you all over town. Tried your house on the phone and your secretary told me he thought you'd gone to a bookshop called the Moonlight—"

Caroline turned to him irritably.

"Do I employ you for your reminiscences?" she snapped. "Are you my tutor or my broker?"

"Your broker," confessed the fur-trimmed man, taken somewhat aback. "I beg your pardon. I came about that phonograph stock. I can sell for a hundred and five."

"Then do it."

"Very well. I thought I'd better—"

"Go sell it. I'm talking to my grandson."

"Very well. I—"

"Goodbye."

"Goodbye, Madame." The fur-trimmed man made a slight bow and hurried in some confusion from the shop.

"As for you," said Caroline, turning to her grandson, "you stay just where you are and be quiet."

She turned to Merlin and included his entire length in a not unfriendly survey. Then she smiled and he found himself smiling too. In an instant they had both broken into a cracked but nonetheless spontaneous chuckle. She seized his arm and hurried him to the other side of the store. There they stopped, faced each other, and gave vent to another long fit of senile glee.

"It's the only way," she gasped in a sort of triumphant malignity. "The only thing that keeps old folks like me happy is the sense that they can make other people step around. To be old and rich and have poor descendants is almost as much fun as to be young and beautiful and have ugly sisters."

"Oh, yes," chuckled Merlin. "I know. I envy you."

She nodded, blinking.

"The last time I was in here, forty years ago," she said, "you were a young man very anxious to kick up your heels."

"I was," he confessed.

"My visit must have meant a good deal to you."

"You have all along," he exclaimed. "I thought—I used to think at first that you were a real person—human, I mean."

She laughed.

"Many men have thought me inhuman."

"But now," continued Merlin excitedly, "I understand. Understanding is allowed to us old people—after nothing much matters. I see now that on a certain night when you danced upon a table-top you were nothing but my romantic yearning for a beautiful and perverse woman."

Her old eyes were far away, her voice no more than the echo of a forgotten dream.

"How I danced that night! I remember."

"You were making an attempt at me. Olive's arms were closing about me and you warned me to be free and keep my measure of youth and irresponsibility. But it seemed like an effect gotten up at the last moment. It came too late."

"You are very old," she said inscrutably. "I did not realize."

"Also I have not forgotten what you did to me when I was thirty-five. You shook me with that traffic tie-up. It was a magnificent effort. The beauty and power you radiated! You became personified even to my wife, and she feared you. For weeks I wanted to slip out of the house at dark and forget the stuffiness of life with music and cocktails and a girl to make me young. But then—I no longer knew how."

"And now you are so very old."

With a sort of awe she moved back and away from him.

"Yes, leave me!" he cried. "You are old also; the spirit withers with the skin. Have you come here only to tell me something I had best forget: that to be old and poor is perhaps more wretched than to be old and rich; to remind me that *my* son hurls my gray failure in my face?"

"Give me my book," she commanded harshly. "Be quick, old man!"

Merlin looked at her once more and then patiently obeyed. He picked up the book and handed it to her, shaking his head when she offered him a bill.

"Why go through the farce of paying me? Once you made me wreck these very premises."

"I did," she said in anger, "and I'm glad. Perhaps there had been enough done to ruin *me*."

She gave him a glance, half disdain, half ill-concealed uneasiness, and with a brisk word to her urban grandson moved toward the door.

Then she was gone—out of his shop—out of his life. The door clicked. With a sigh he turned and walked brokenly back toward the glass partition that enclosed the yellowed accounts of many years as well as the mellowed, wrinkled Miss McCracken.

Merlin regarded her parched, cobwebbed face with an odd sort of pity. She, at any rate, had had less from life than he. No rebellious, romantic spirit popping out unbidden had, in its memorable moments, given her life a zest and a glory.

Then Miss McGracken looked up and spoke to him:

"Still a spunky old piece, isn't she?"

Merlin started.

"Who?"

"Old Alicia Dare. Mrs. Thomas Allerdyce she is now, of course; has been, these thirty years."

"What? I don't understand you." Merlin sat down suddenly in his swivel chair; his eyes were wide.

"Why, surely, Mr. Grainger, you can't tell me that you've forgotten her, when for ten years she was the most notorious character in New York. Why, one time when she was the correspondent in the Throckmorton divorce case she attracted so much attention on Fifth Avenue that there was a traffic tie-up. Didn't you read about it in the papers."

"I never used to read the papers." His ancient brain was whirring.

"Well, you can't have forgotten the time she came in here and ruined the business. Let me tell you I came near asking Mr. Moonlight Quill for my salary, and clearing out."

"Do you mean, that—that you *saw* her?"

"Saw her! How could I help it with the racket that went on. Heaven knows Mr. Moonlight Quill didn't like it either but of course *he* didn't say anything. He was daffy about her and she could twist him around her little finger. The second he opposed one of her whims she'd threaten to tell his wife on him. Served him right. The idea of that man falling for a pretty adventuress! Of course he was never rich enough for *her* even though the shop paid well in those days."

"But when I saw her." stammered Merlin, "that is, when I *thought* saw her, she lived with her mother."

"Mother, trash!" said Miss McCracken indignantly. "She had a woman there she called Aunty, who was no more related to her than I am. Oh, she was a bad one—but clever. Right after the Throckmorton divorce case she married Thomas Allerdyce, and made herself secure for life."

"Who was she?" cried Merlin. "For God's sake what was she—a witch?"

"Why, she was Alicia Dare, the dancer, of course. In those days you couldn't pick up a paper without finding her picture."

Merlin sat very quiet, his brain suddenly fatigued and stilled. He was an old man now indeed, so old that it was impossible for him to dream of ever having been young, so old that the glamour was gone out of the world, passing not into the faces of children and into the persistent comforts of warmth and life, but passing out of the range of sight and feeling. He was never to smile again or to sit in a long reverie when spring evenings wafted the cries of children in at his window until gradually they became the friends of his boyhood out there, urging him to come and play before the last dark came down. He was too old now even for memories.

That night he sat at supper with his wife and son, who had used him for their blind purposes. Olive said:

"Don't sit there like a death's-head. Say something."

"Let him sit quiet," growled Arthur. "If you encourage him he'll tell us a story we've heard a hundred times before."

Merlin went up-stairs very quietly at nine o'clock. When he was in his room and had closed the door tight he stood by it for a moment, his thin limbs trembling. He knew now that he had always been a fool.

"O Russet Witch!"

But it was too late. He had angered Providence by resisting too many temptations. There was nothing left but heaven, where he would meet only those who, like him, had wasted earth.